D1132010

Also by Peggy Tibbetts

The Road to Weird
Rumors of War
PFC Liberty Stryker
Hurricane Katrina

Letters to Juniper

By Peggy Tibbetts

"Tibbetts is a skilled and masterful writer. This is a book you will want to share with your children, your parents, and your friends."–Natalie R. Collins, author of *Wives and Sisters, Behind Closed Doors, The Fourth World, Sister Wife,* and *Twisted Sister*

For Ema, who said, "Don't you dare change a thing."

Acknowledgements

The National Center for Missing & Exploited Children was established by Congress in 1984. Since then it has assisted law enforcement in the recovery of more than 145,600 children. The organization works in cooperation with the U.S. Department of Justice's office of Juvenile Justice and Delinquency Prevention. To learn more about NCMEC, visit www.missingkids.com. Their tireless efforts on behalf of children everywhere deserve our most profound gratitude.

Once a story is written it can take on a life of its own. *Letters to Juniper* is one of those stories. I'm grateful to everyone who read it and believed in it, especially Natalie Collins because she never forgot. A special thank you to Alison Kentta for giving this story legs when she awarded it first prize in YA Fiction.com's "First Three" middle grade contest in May 2007. And to Calista, my tireless reader, this is the one you haven't read. I'm grateful for all my readers who—like me—have waited patiently for the stars to align and this orphan to find a home. Thanks to Sisterhood Publications. This *feels* like home.

Friday, August 2

Dear Juniper,

You probably don't remember me. My name is Sarah Smith. I've been thinking about you a lot lately.

We were best friends around six years ago. We lived next door to each other. In Florida. I'll never forget the name of the street we lived on. Bird of Paradise Lane. It stayed with me after all this time. I'm not even sure if you still live there anymore.

At first I couldn't remember the name of the town. I knew it was Fort M-something. So I looked it up on the map of Florida. I found Fort Myers and I'm pretty sure that's the one.

Today is my birthday. I'm 12. Hannah and the Slocumbs came by for supper. Hannah is my best friend. You'd really like her. She's 12, too.

I picked my own bouquet of zinnias for the dinner table. We had venison meat loaf, new potatoes and peas from the garden, and the first pick of our sweet corn. Yummy!

There was carrot cake for dessert with 12 candles for my birthday. I blew out every candle except one. But I don't have a boyfriend. So it doesn't count.

The Slocumbs gave me a six-pack of spiral notebooks from Sam's Club. From my own family I got a plaid flannel shirt. Oversize. Unlined. Just the way I like them. Also two more Nancy Drew Books for my set. Plus some underwear, socks, and one pack each of Bic pens and pencils from Sam's Club.

As birthdays go, it was okay. I've had worse. Like when I was seven. I spent my birthday alone, babysitting my little brother, Abraham. Do you remember him? Daddy was working. He forgot all about it. And Abraham didn't know any better. He was four then.

My best birthday was when I was six. Do you remember the pony rides at my party? You should. You were there. We had so much fun. It was at our old house on Bird of Paradise Lane, with Mommy. I had one of those bakery cakes with the sweet, gooey frosting decorated like Mickey Mouse. There was a ton of kids there.

You must be 12 by now. When is your birthday? I can't remember. Please tell me whenever you write back.

I don't know when these letters will ever get mailed to you. Daddy takes care of all our mail. And I'm pretty sure he won't send any letters to Florida for me. So I'm writing them in one of the spiral notebooks I got today. That way I can save them up. Next time I get to town, I'll mail them myself.

It must seem to you like I left very suddenly back then. We never even got to say goodbye. I never got the chance to explain what happened.

You remember how we used to go visit Daddy at his apartment, after the divorce. Well, this one weekend while we were with Daddy, our mommy was killed in a car accident. But I think you probably found out about that, since we were neighbors and all.

Anyway, we went to live with Daddy. We lived in a camper until I was nine. First in Georgia, then Missouri, or maybe Michigan. I get those two mixed up. Now we live near Bonners Ferry, Idaho.

Daddy built our house up here on Meadow Ridge. If you ever come to Bonners Ferry to visit, you'll never be able to find this place. You have to take a whole bunch of twists and turns on Forest Service roads. We're on KNF (stands for Kaniksu National Forest) No. 247. Everyone just calls it Meadow Ridge Road.

We don't get mail delivery up here. Daddy has a box at the post office in Bonners Ferry. If you ever get my letters, you should write back to me at General Delivery, Bonners Ferry, ID, 83805. I'll ask Mrs. Beekman at the post ffice to save them for me.

Abraham is nine now. And we have a new mom. Her name is Shelly. I don't call her Mom unless Daddy makes me. I like her okay and all. She's more like a stepsister. My real mommy was older than her. Shelly's 24. She has a boy, Travis. He's six. And she and Daddy have a baby boy, Joseph. He's almost two.

Yeller is our yellow lab. Trained retriever. I was the one who named him Old Yeller, after the dog in the book. But everyone just calls him Yeller for short. We take him bird hunting.

I have a cat, too. She's a brown tabby. We got her from the Slocumbs when she was a kitten. I call her Ginny. But nobody else does. Daddy refuses to call her that. Says it's an ugly name. I don't know why. So he started calling her Cat, and now everybody else does too.

It's way past dark. I am writing to you by candlelight. I don't want Daddy to catch me. So I best be off to the outhouse with my faithful flashlight in hand and then back to bed.

Good night, Juniper. Wherever you are.

Your friend,

Sarah

Thursday, August 8

Dear Juniper,

Boy am I beat! Fell asleep during Bible study tonight. We don't have a TV. Instead we have Bible study almost every single night.

I remember those shows like *Sesame Street* and *Mr. Rogers' Neighborhood*. Are they still out there? Sometimes I miss TV. But Daddy says it brainwashes you. He says it's all government propaganda. I think it means lies or something. Also there's too much sex and violence.

We don't have a telephone either. There's no phone lines this far back in the mountains. And, as you might have guessed by the end of my last letter, we don't have an indoor bathroom. That's what the outhouse is for. No running water either. Me and the boys haul water up from the spring on the east trail. There's no washing machine. No dryer. Me and Shelly wash the clothes by hand and hang them on clotheslines. We take our baths in the tub out in the birthing shed.

I guess this might seem primitive to you, compared to your house in Florida. Daddy says we have to live this way because we're Separatists. He says modern conveniences cost too much money and only make us like slaves to the government.

The chicken coop is also out back. We have 12 chickens. Shelly calls them her prize Rhode Island Reds. Don't ask me why they're called Reds, because they're actually brown. We don't eat those chickens. Shelly says their eggs are more valuable than their meat.

At first they just ran around out in the yard, because she wanted them to be free-range chickens. But it was practically impossible to find the eggs. That's why Daddy built the chicken coop for them. Shelly sells the extra eggs to our friends at the Camp. Me and Shelly are the only ones allowed to collect eggs. The boys break too many. And Shelly claims they get the chickens all riled up.

The reason I'm so tired is because I was out in the garden with the boys, picking beans and cucumbers all morning. Then in the afternoon, me and Shelly made pickles and canned beans. It's a ton of work. Did you ever make pickles? I had to scrub the cucumbers with a brush, cut up the big ones and put them all in the vinegar brine Shelly stirred up.

Travis and Abraham called it her witches brew. She chewed their butts and sent them up to the loft in the heat of the afternoon. Which left little old me to snap all those beans! I don't know why she can't figure it out. Those two brats do that stuff on purpose. Just to get out of work. She's so blind. She plays right into it. But if I dare say one thing about her precious Travis, she blames it all on Abraham.

"He leads Travis around by the nose," Shelly said.

All I said was, "Travis follows his own nose into trouble." And she shooed me back out to the garden to pick more beans.

Picking beans is the worst! The bushes were full of daddy longlegs. Gross! While crouching out there in the sweltering sun, I thought about you and your house in Florida. You had the best swing set! It had a barrel slide—all the neighbor kids came over to your house to play. You and me played Barbies quite a lot back then. I don't play with Barbies anymore. Mostly I read books from the Camp Library. Sometimes I buy them at rummage sales.

Do you remember my mommy? She was so nice. She used to give us juice boxes and Oreo cookies. Do you still get those? They were the best. With white cream in the middle. Makes my mouth water.

We don't get Oreos anymore. Shelly bakes all the cookies. We're not supposed to have sugar. So she makes the cookies with honey. They aren't crunchy like Oreos. She makes raisin and sunflower-seed cookies. They're soft and squishy. Besides I hate raisins. The boys shape them into balls and play catch with them. She gets pretty riled up about that. But they eat them eventually. Boys'll eat anything. So it doesn't really matter if Shelly's cookies taste yucky.

The only juice we ever have is apple cider we make in the fall. Daddy has his own cider press. After all the canning's done in August, Shelly doesn't want any part of making cider. So me and Daddy always do it. It's kind of fun washing and sorting the apples, then watching him run them through the press. To tell you the truth though, I get kind of sick of drinking boring old apple cider year after year.

Anyway, we canned a grand total of 52 pints of beans today. Tomorrow the pickles will be ready to pack in jars. After all the picking and canning, I'm really tired. Think I'll call it quits. Good night.

Your friend,

Sarah

Wednesday, August 14

Dear Juniper,

Everyone else is asleep. Ginny the cat's here beside me, kneading the quilt with her paws and purring loudly.

Abraham found my notebook of letters to you. He said he didn't read them. I think he's telling the truth because he hates to read. I hid the notebook under my mattress. But he told Daddy on me. The little geek. Daddy chewed my butt about it tonight.

Daddy: "I don't want you writing letters to anybody in Florida. Hear me?"

Me: "But I don't see what's so wrong with it."

Daddy: "Florida's an evil place."

Me: "But I don't remember it like that. Thinking about Florida helps me remember my mommy. Sometimes I really miss her."

Daddy: "The Bible says if you are with Yashua, old things are passed away and all things become new. You have a new mother now. Are you with Yashua, Sarah?"

Me: "I guess so."

Daddy: "Someday you'll understand the path of Yashua's redemption. And how I reclaimed what was rightfully mine back then. For now, you go on and fetch those letters. Then toss them in the cook stove. I'm waiting."

Don't panic! I fooled him and put my spelling notebook in the fire instead.

Anyway, I have to be extra careful no one finds these letters. That's real hard considering I share this loft with the boys, too. Don't get me wrong. It's a big loft. And I have one wall of bookshelves for a divider. But there's no door. No privacy. I have to hide everything from those geeks.

I apologize in advance if my penmanship gets sloppy sometimes. Please bear with me. It looks like my letter writing is going to have to come late at night after everyone else has gone to bed. And when I'm tired myself, as well.

I do have an old manual typewriter I bought at a rummage sale last spring for two dollars. The X key is missing, but otherwise it works great. I would love to type these letters on it, but the clicking of the keys would make too much noise after bedtime. Quiet hands guiding pencil on paper is really the only option I have.

Tomatoes are ripe. Today we started picking and canning them. I swear, sometimes it seems like the only reason grownups have kids is so they have plenty of workers.

Ginny the cat keeps grabbing the pencil out of my hand. She's making it impossible to write. And she's also making me giggle. I'd better quit before somebody wakes up. Anyway, I'm beat. I can't even keep my eyes open.

Good night Juniper. Wherever you are.

Your friend,

Sarah

Tuesday, September 3

Dear Juniper,

We had a very brief Bible study and prayer tonight. Trouble visited our house today. Two men drove up this morning in a black Jeep. I thought maybe they came from the Camp down in Hayden Lake. But Daddy didn't act like he recognized them. He told us later they were federal agents.

Daddy ordered us kids to stay indoors. Then he slung his rifle over his shoulder and walked outside. Shelly carried Joseph out the front door after him. As soon as the agents saw Daddy's gun, they jumped out of the Jeep, drew their handguns, and hid behind the open doors. It was really scary.

The first agent hollered, "Drop your gun, Dalton!" (That's my Daddy's name.)

Shelly hollered back, "You wouldn't shoot down a man in front of his own family now. Would you?"

First agent: "Mrs. Smith, put the baby down. Then raise your hands in the air. Nice and slow."

Joseph started bawling. Probably because Shelly was squeezing him to death. Daddy went ahead and laid his rifle down on the ground. But Shelly stood firm. I have no idea why she was acting so crazy.

The agents stepped out from behind the Jeep's door, their weapons still pointed at Daddy and Shelly.

First agent: "I said put the baby down, Mrs. Smith."

Shelly: "What for?"

Second agent: "You carrying a concealed weapon?"

Shelly: "I'm carrying my son."

First agent: "You and your son go on back inside the house, Mrs. Smith. Our business is with Dalton."

Shelly put Joseph down and held his hand. Both agents rushed over and frisked Daddy and her. Then they started talking so low I couldn't hear what they were saying.

Of course with all the excitement, the boys had to go and pee off the back porch. I had to go, too, so I sneaked out the back door. The outhouse is up against a stand of pine trees between the house and the birthing shed. The house and outbuildings, except the chicken coop, are situated in a semicircle around the driveway. Daddy built them that way on purpose so he can see who's coming no matter where he is. Daddy doesn't like surprises.

From my vantage point at the outhouse I could see one of the men wore a plaid shirt and vest. The other had on a brown leather jacket. They looked just like anybody else. But I still wasn't close enough to hear anything. So I darted over to the birthing shed. From the nearest corner I could hear just about everything they said.

First agent: "We're not asking you to do anything out of the ordinary. Just go to the meetings like you always do. We'll provide you with the recording device. Won't even have to make a special trip. I'll meet you at the Sandpoint Diner afterward. Then just hand over the tape. Clean and simple."

Daddy: "To hell with that!"

Second agent: "That warrant's for real, Dalton. It's sitting in your post office box down in Bonners Ferry right this very minute. You either cooperate and give us the information on the Order, or go to jail for the sale of illegal weapons. It's your decision."

Daddy: "You got that much right. So you might as well arrest me on the spot. I don't plan on being an informant for the government. That's for damn sure."

First agent: "Don't be so quick to refuse. There's good money in it for you. A lot. More than you made on that gun deal."

Second agent: "From the looks of this place and knowing you got four kids to support I'd say you'd be wise to take your time. Think it over some more."

Daddy (yelling): "If you didn't come here to arrest me, then get the hell off my property!"

Second agent: "We'll be in touch."

They climbed in the Jeep and rumbled down the steep ravine that is our driveway. Good thing they had four-wheel drive. It rained last night and there's some huge chuck holes in the dirt road.

I guess I'd better explain what this is all about. Daddy happens to be a gunsmith. He fixes and sells guns. Sometimes he gets orders through the mail. Mostly he does business with the men down at the Camp in Hayden Lake. He goes to meetings there, too.

From what Daddy told us, one of those men who came here today had offered Daddy extra money awhile back, if he sawed off a couple shotguns for him. And Daddy said since us kids are always growing out of our clothes and shoes, he needed the extra money. That man turned out to be a federal agent. Now there's a warrant for Daddy's arrest waiting for him in our post office box.

Usually he goes to Bonners Ferry every day to pick up mail and supplies. Today he stayed home.

There's something else I need to tell you. That agent kept calling Shelly "Mrs. Smith." But she and Daddy aren't really married. They didn't have an actual wedding or anything. Daddy calls it a common-law marriage. He doesn't believe in any other kind of marriage anymore. I guess that's because of the divorce.

Daddy says, "A man signs away everything he owns when he signs a marriage license. The Bible says when the resurrection comes, they neither marry, nor are given in marriage."

As I'm writing this tonight, I can hear Daddy and Shelly talking downstairs.

Daddy: "Man can't make an honest living anymore without the government sticking their noses in where they don't belong."

Shelly: "Are you going to get them information on the Order?"

Daddy: "Hell no. But I don't want Fisher or Slocumb, or anyone else knowing the offer was even made. Just get them all riled up over nothing. So don't you breathe a word of it. Hear me?"

Shelly: "Dalton. Go to the Camp. Meet with the Order. They'll find you a lawyer. After all, they need your guns."

Daddy: "I don't need a lawyer."

Shelly: "But that agent set you up. A good lawyer can help you prove that."

Daddy: "You know as well as I do how lawyers love publicity. It's a sure bet they'll call in the TV cameras. Turn us into sideshow freaks."

Shelly: "But we could use that publicity to blow the whistle on the feds."

Daddy: "I'm not blowing the whistle on anybody. Just leave it alone. I won't make our lives into a living hell."

Shelly: "What about that warrant?"

Daddy: "The way I see it, if I don't set foot in that post office to pick up my mail, then that warrant's non-deliverable. Not one damn thing they can do about it."

Sorry about the cursing. I was just repeating what Daddy said.

And I just realized what this all means. He's not going to the post office anymore. This ruins my whole plan! Now I don't know how I'm going to send you these letters. I was going to go along with him to the post office and take this notebook.

I thought I would buy one of those envelopes already stamped. Then I'd rip out the letters, stuff them in the envelope, and address it to you. Daddy gives us each fifty cents a week for allowance. So I've been saving up my quarters. But if he doesn't even go to the post office, then I don't have a prayer of mailing these myself.

I'm too riled up about this to write anymore tonight. I'll write back when I figure out a new plan.

Your friend,

Sarah

Friday, September 6

Dear Juniper,

Me again. Not one single plan of mine has worked out yet.

Daddy went to Bonners Ferry yesterday. I thought if I could go along, I'd sneak over to the post office and mail your letters while he was at the IGA Store. No such luck. He said I had to stay home in case he ran into trouble. Shelly got to go along instead. I had to babysit. Rats!

Mr. Fisher and his son, Karl, were here this morning. Shelly sold them six cartons of eggs. Mr. Fisher's a member of the Order. Daddy goes to the meetings with him at the Camp.

Some of the members, like the Fishers and Slocumbs actually live there. At the Camp. We don't because Daddy doesn't believe in belonging to any groups. He says the government keeps files on all those people who do.

Sometimes we go down there to the Church of Jesus Christ Christian on Sundays. I don't exactly know what religion it is. It's part of the Aryan Nation. We go to Sunday School there, too. We have to drive almost two hours to get to the Camp, so it takes up pretty much the whole day. Afterward, there's always a pot luck dinner.

The Order is a group of men. Mr. Fisher and Mr. Slocumb are both members. The Grand Master of the Aryan Nation is Mr. Champion. He's never been up to our place. But I've seen him lots of times down at the Camp. Even though Daddy's not a member of their Order, they usually invite him to the meetings. Except he doesn't always agree with everything they say. He says the only reason he goes along is because they have the manpower to fight the Revolution. He believes that's what this country needs. And of course he does business with them.

Daddy and Shelly talked to Mr. Fisher about the warrant at the post office. But they didn't talk about the agents who came here. And they left out the stuff about Daddy being an informant.

Mr. Fisher: "What are you going to do?"

Daddy: "Nothing."

Mr. Fisher: "You know, the Order can bring an attorney up here. From Boise."

27

Daddy: "I don't want some Boise potato head calling in the TV tabloids and exposing my wife and kids to their garbage. I won't be made an example of. Just leave it alone."

I was giggling about the potato head remark when Karl came over and shoved me behind the garage. He just wanted to smoke his cigarette in front of somebody. He's 15. A real pain. He'd be good looking if he didn't shave off all his hair. Or wear camouflage green all the time.

I told him, "If Daddy catches you smoking back here, he'll chew your butt."

He flicked his cigarette and sassed, "I'd consider it an honor to get my butt chewed by your daddy. He's got more guts than any man I know. Spittin in the feds' faces like that."

Then he spit on the ground. For effect, I guess. I wasn't impressed. "What do you mean?"

Karl: "You know damn well what I mean. The feds were here and offered to drop those charges if your daddy'll spy on the Order for them."

Well, you can just imagine I was beside myself wondering how in the world he heard about that. I thought we weren't supposed to talk about it. But I didn't dare let on I knew what he was talking about.

Me: "Where did you hear such a story?"

Karl: "Everybody knows. Man, what I'd a given to be here and see him lob a wad right in that sonofabitch's eyeball."

Me: "That's a lie! My daddy never spit in that agent's eye. You think you're such a big shot Nazi."

Karl carries his rifle in a sling, like a soldier. He adjusted it right then, for more effect, I guess. Then he said, "I don't think. I know."

He stamped out his cigarette and goose-stepped away around the corner. He tries to act like such a skinhead.

And if you happen to be thinking about the last candle on my birthday cake right now, Juniper, don't even dream for one second there's even a remote possibility he might be my boyfriend. Ugh.

Anyway, I can't believe I actually thought about asking him to take your letters to the post office for me. My plan was to give him the letters and if he refused, I'd threaten to tell on him for smoking behind the garage. As you can see, today wasn't exactly the perfect time to bring out some letters for him to send to Florida. I hope you understand.

Your friend,

Sarah

Wednesday, September 11

Dear Juniper,

I guess you're back in school after summer vacation. And you're probably wondering why I'm not. I don't go to school. Neither do the boys.

The government says there's no place for prayer in school. So Daddy says school is no place for his kids. We do homeschooling which is why I'm late writing to you. We had a long history lesson tonight before Bible study. Daddy was going on and on about the American Revolution.

He read aloud this quote from Thomas Paine: "It is not a field of a few acres of ground, but a cause, that we are defending, and whether we defeat the enemy in one battle, or by degrees, the consequences will be the same."

"Our cause is freedom. This is Armageddon," Daddy said. "We will fight this holy war for freedom by degrees. And defend our right to live life the way we choose."

Daddy believes homeschooling is better than public school. For one thing, he says Idaho schools are the worst in the country. Karl told me there's gangs. Drugs. You probably know all about that. If you still live in Florida.

Daddy says, "There's only one place worse than Idaho. And that's Florida. The devil's playground."

I'll pray for your safety, Juniper.

What grade are you in this year? I don't even know what grade I'm in anymore. I used to know, but I've lost track. The last time I went to school was in Florida. I don't really remember much else about it, except I know you were there. I think I was in first grade when Mommy died. But I never finished that grade.

It's hard to explain homeschooling. It's not like school at all. Shelly is like our teacher. For reading. Daddy doesn't know I'm the one who taught *her* how to read. She didn't even know how. Maybe Daddy's right about the schools here. Shelly graduated from high school and she never learned how to read.

Daddy says there are lessons to be learned every day. So we have to learn how to do everything. We have math workbooks, history books and science books. Reading is my favorite thing. And I also like writing.

Every month we have to compose an essay about what significant thing we learned. I like to type all my essays on clean white paper. Shelly doesn't know how to type either.

Last month I wrote about making pickles. This month I'm going to write about Thomas Paine. He said some cool stuff about freedom.

My candle is burning low. Good night Juniper.

Your friend,

Sarah

Friday, September 20

Dear Juniper,

All of a sudden, guns are a really big deal around here. My daddy stores extra guns and ammunition for the Order, up here on our property. I guess I never paid much attention before all this happened. That's always been strictly Daddy's business. Now he frets about it. Because he says the feds might come snooping around.

Everyone in my family owns a gun. Except Joseph, of course. Mine is a .22 rifle. I use it for grouse hunting.

I learned to shoot it when I was seven. We were living in the camper in Georgia. Sometimes Daddy had to leave us alone so he could go to work. I had to learn how to shoot, in case of trouble. Except he never said what the trouble was.

But I'm warning you, don't even try to shoot a gun by yourself. Knocked me flat on my butt. I didn't like it one bit, at first. Gave me the worst headache. But I'm bigger and stronger now. It's not so heavy. And I have to clean the dang gun after every time I shoot it. It's a real pain.

Hunting and shooting is just something Daddy's always expected me to do. I refuse to hunt deer or elk. I hate gutting and skinning such a huge, magnificent animal. And then dragging it out of the mountains. It's gross. I mean it's so—dead!

With grouse hunting it's different. If you ask me, there's not much difference between a live grouse and a dead one. Except for when it's alive, it's standing up on its spindly little legs instead of laying sideways. If I snuck up behind one, I could just as easily club it over the head, rather than waste a bullet. They are that dumb.

Besides, if I don't go along with the guys when they go bird hunting, then Shelly makes a whole list of chores for me to do. Ugh. On the other hand, I'll gladly wash windows to keep from cutting up Bambi's mother with a hacksaw.

This is hunting season, so Daddy is especially busy with his gun business. We went grouse hunting today, in fact. I really do enjoy being out in the forest. It's so peaceful. The birds were singing. Ground squirrels were chattering. I even spotted a bighorn sheep crossing Meadow Creek.

Abraham shot the first grouse today. Travis was so jealous. Secretly I was especially happy for my little brother. Seems like Travis always gets the attention. For once it was Abraham's turn. Then Shelly went and cooked the grouse meat into stew.

I said, "You should've roasted the whole bird to show it off for Abraham."

She replied, "Abraham is a bad marksman. His shot ruined half the meat."

Well it looked like a clean shot to me. But what do I know?

Anyway, it doesn't look like this whole business about the warrant is going to blow over any time soon, like I was hoping. Fishers and Slocumbs keep coming by with gossip about the feds being spotted everywhere from Bonners Ferry to Hayden Lake. Word's out they'll arrest Daddy, if they catch him off the property.

Even if I can't get to town, at least I've been able to get out of this house and into the woods for a while. I only hope my hunting tales don't bore you to death.

Your friend,

Sarah

Saturday, September 28

Dear Juniper,

I have the most exciting news! There's a Harvest Dance at the Camp on Saturday, November 2. Daddy said we might be able to go!

Hannah and the Slocumbs came by today. They needed eggs. We had plenty to spare. Millie is Hannah's baby sister. She's five. We played with her and Joseph most of the time, so the moms could drink coffee and talk.

While we were up in the loft, Hannah told me all about the Harvest Dance. "I've a got a secret. But I'm not supposed to say anything before my mom asks first."

Me: "Does it have something to do with the dance?"

Hannah: "No. It's about afterward. I want you to come and stay for a sleepover."

Me "Oh wow! They just have to say yes. I haven't been anywhere in months."

I could hardly wait to hear their answer. Daddy and Mr. Slocumb spent the day hauling in pickup loads of firewood. Then the Slocumbs stayed for supper.

Afterward the grown-ups were sitting around the table and Mrs. Slocumb finally said, "Now don't forget about that Harvest Dance. I'm counting on you and Dalton to put in some time at my raffle booth."

Shelly: "We'll be there. You can count on us."

Mrs. Slocumb: "Hannah was hoping Sarah could stay for a sleepover. We'll bring her back on Sunday, if you promise to save me a few dozen eggs.

You can't even imagine how excited I am. Finally I might get to leave these prison grounds! And for the Harvest Dance, of all things. This is so incredibly fantastic!

The only catch is what Daddy said. "It's between Yashua and Sarah whether or not she gets to stay over after the dance. We'll see what happens during the next few weeks."

Of course Daddy and Shelly will be watching me like hawks. So it's my job to butter up both of them extra special. Stay out of trouble. The whole routine. Come Harvest Dance, they'll have no choice but to let me stay with Hannah.

Speaking of Hannah, she helped me pick out black material with pink and white flowers from the trunk underneath the sewing machine. I'm going to make myself a new skirt. I asked Shelly if she'd let me borrow her white silk blouse with the huge collar.

"We'll see," she said.

At the Camp they do the country line dance. There's this one part where all the women put their hand in their pockets and twirl around. I gotta have pockets.

Oh Juniper, so much excitement all in one day. I'm exhausted. My candle is nothing more than a pool of burning wax.

Good night Juniper. Wherever you are.

Your friend,

Sarah

Friday, October 4

Dear Juniper,

Mr. Fisher and Karl showed up here before dawn. We all went duck hunting up on Priest Lake. Shelly stayed home with Joseph.

I have to tell you, Karl was acting very strange today. I don't know what to make of it. He was sitting next to me on a log by the lake shore. We had Yeller with us. We were waiting for Daddy, Mr. Fisher, and the boys to flush out some ducks from the blind behind us.

Karl asked me, "Seen any feds sneaking around your property lately?"

Me: "Oh sure. The place is just crawling with them. Can't you tell?"

Karl: "Tell me more."

But I just laughed at him. "Karl! I'm kidding. Nobody comes up to our place. Except you and your dad. And sometimes the Slocumbs."

He shrugged. "Whatever you say."

41

Me: "Speaking of the Slocumbs, I'm going to spend the night at Hannah's after the Harvest Dance."

Karl: "That's interesting."

With that, the orange October sky erupted into the beating of duck wings and quacking. A shot rang out behind us and one fluttered to the water. I released my hold on Yeller's collar and he splashed into the silent lake, hot after the kill. It was truly an awesome sight.

Afterward Karl had to smoke his cigarette. While we hiked back into the trees, the conversation sort of went like this:

Karl: "My sister's getting married in June."

Me: "Ruthie? She's only 17."

Karl: "She'll be 18 in January."

Me: "Still. She's so young. Is it Aaron Johnson?"

Karl: "Who else? One fine young Nazi."

Me: "But he's a ton older than her."

Karl: "Six years. That's not much. Anyway Aryans marry young. My Dad says I need to start keeping my eyes open for wife material."

Me: "Well, you're definitely too young to get married."

Karl: "Yeah. But when you're 18, I'll be 21. That's old enough."

I guess I must've blushed. It's hard to tell outdoors in the crisp Autumn air. To think he has even considered marrying me. I know I've complained about what a shameless Nazi he can be, but I have to tell you, when Karl said that to me, I was kind of flattered.

Anyway, I shot a pintail today. Later on, it was Karl's and my job to walk the lake shore and fetch the decoys. Daddy, Mr. Fisher, and the boys met us at the roadside, where they parked the trucks. On the way, Yeller scared up the pintail in the reeds along shore.

"Go for it!" Karl shouted.

I just reacted. Clipped off a shot just as the duck took wing. Caught him in the neck. Yeller plucked him out of the water for me. The guys all made a huge fuss. I don't know who was prouder, Daddy or Karl.

It wasn't the first pintail I ever shot, by any means. But on the ride back home, I knew it could easily be the last. Staring at those beautiful feathers I thought about how he was minding his own business in his little pond, on the edge of the lake. Then I invaded his territory, scared him out of hiding, and shot him.

I started thinking of what Daddy says about freedom. That poor duck had all the freedom he ever wanted, until I came along today. Maybe I'm no different than those feds who want to arrest my Daddy. And I sure don't want to be like them.

Of course I kept those thoughts to myself. Back home I let Abraham dress the duck for me. I didn't want anymore to do with it. Abraham didn't mind one bit.

I wonder if guys ever feel this way. Or if it's just a girl thing. Juniper, I don't know if you've ever killed anything before. But I have. Plenty of times. Truthfully I never thought much about it. It's just something I was supposed to do.

Daddy says, "The Bible says rise, kill and eat. Every man is free to choose how best to live his life. And this is the way we choose."

I'm afraid my heart's not in it anymore.

Before, the grouse or the duck was always a trophy for dinner. In this family, when it's your clean shot that puts food on the table, it's a big deal. But now it doesn't seem so simple.

I wish you were my next door neighbor still. We could have our own sleepover. Put our heads together under the covers and talk all night. I miss you. Wherever you are.

Your friend,

Sarah

Monday, October 14

Dear Juniper,

Shelly's holding the Harvest Dance over my head like a live hand grenade. I worked like a dog all last week. She made me do everything around here. I can't begin to describe what she's putting me through. Feed the baby. Hang out the wash. Peel potatoes. Gather eggs. Sew buttons. Like I'm her slave. Tonight she actually sat down and played puzzles on the floor with Joseph. I had to wash dishes all by myself.

Me: "Who's going to haul water? I can't lift those jugs. They're too heavy."

Shelly: "Just take the dish pan over to the jug and pour some water into it. Then add hot water from the stove. Figure it out, Miss Smarty Pants."

Wicked Old Witch. She's just jealous because I get to stay late at the dance and sleep over at Hannah's, but she'll have to go home early with Daddy and the boys.

Last night I heard her begging him, "Please, Dalton. Let's stay over for church on Sunday. Be good for the kids to get to Sunday School."

Daddy: "That may be true. But there's no place for us to stay."

Shelly persisted, mapping out her plan. "I figured it out. We can split up. I'm sure the Slocumbs won't mind if me and Joseph stay along with Sarah. Then you and the boys can stay with the Fishers. It'll be safer that way, too."

Daddy: "Can't risk it. That's too long in one place. Won't take the feds any time at all to figure out where to find me."

Shelly: "Please. Just think it over."

Daddy: "I've thought about it all I'm going to. The answer is no."

Anyway, I've been frantically trying to get my skirt done during the mornings after chores, and before I have to fix lunch. I'm afraid I won't get it done in time. All we have is an old pedal sewing machine. Takes forever, and I'm not the best seamstress.

Hasn't allowed me any extra time for letter writing. That's for sure. But I figure once the dance is over with, I'll have all the time in the world to write letters again. And tons more stuff to write about.

I'm going to take this notebook with me when I go to Hannah's. Just in case I can talk her into mailing them for me. Keep your fingers crossed. You might be getting a fistful of letters in your mailbox really soon. Wherever you are.

Your friend,

Sarah

Thursday, October 31

Dear Juniper,

Happy Halloween!

Aryans don't believe in celebrating Halloween. They believe it's devil worship. "Pagan holiday" is the phrase Daddy always uses. So he agrees with them on that subject.

I can remember our last Halloween with mommy in Florida. I was the Little Mermaid, from the movie. Abraham wore a purple Barney costume. We went to a party at our school, where we paraded around in our costumes. Then we went trick-or-treating around the neighborhood. I'm almost positive you were with us. It was so much fun. There wasn't anything evil or pagan about it. We got a ton of candy.

Tomorrow is All Saints' Day. We each have to choose one of the saints, then we're supposed to read a chapter in the Bible written by him. I always pick St. Jude because it's a short chapter. Then we pray to Yashua for the saints to deliver us from the evil in this world. Of course I'm going to pray for the feds to go away and leave my daddy alone.

Anyway, I can hardly wait for Saturday. The Harvest Dance is going to be so much fun. Daddy finally said I can sleep over at Hannah's. Lucky me!

Your friend,

Sarah

Sunday, November 3

Dear Juniper,

Surprise! It's Sunday already. Have I been the busy one, or what? This was, by far, the most exciting weekend of my entire life! I didn't even get home until this afternoon.

The Harvest Dance was super fun. That's my new word. Super. All the kids at the Camp say it. It was held in the Hall of Nations. There was a band, the Storm Troopers. Three guys playing a keyboard, a fiddle, and a guitar. Of course I danced the country line dance with my hands in the pockets of my new skirt. Twirling with the best of them.

The food there was unbelievable. Caramel apples. Popcorn balls. Pumpkin breads. Cider and fruit punch. Carrots, celery, and broccoli with dip. Brown bread and spinach dip. Trays full of cheeses and smoked meats. And more casseroles than you could ever imagine.

Also, I have to tell you I never realized how famous my daddy has become. So many folks came over and talked to him. I lost count. He was like a celebrity. People said he's a hero because he refused to pick up that warrant. They even started a legal defense fund for him. Everyone wanted him to make a speech, but he graciously bowed out. I have to admit, I was kind of disappointed. Like everyone else, I really wanted to hear him speak. But Daddy's never liked being in the spotlight.

Because of the long drive home, Daddy, Shelly, and the boys left before the dance was over. Of course I was the lucky one who got to stay later with Hannah and the Slocumbs.

The best part of the whole night was when Karl walked me and Hannah home from the Hall. The Camp is sort of like a little village. The Slocumbs' house is there. It was almost midnight. There was a light mist in the air and the wind had started to pick up. Hannah was cold, so she ran inside as soon as we got there.

Karl grabbed the sleeve of my jacket and held me back. I shivered, but not from the cold. I wondered if maybe he just wanted to talk. Or something.

But I didn't wonder for long. He pulled the collar of my jacket up around my neck. Then he kissed my forehead.

Karl: "You're a good dancer. For such a little girl."

Me: "I'm not a little girl."

Then he kissed me on the lips!

Karl: "Not anymore."

Again he kissed my lips.

Karl: "Let's you and me go steady."

I couldn't stop shivering. So all I said was, "O-k-kay."

"That's a good girl," was all he said.

He kissed me once more. And he left. Can you believe I acted so stupid?

Hannah and I stayed up and talked all night. She is such a super friend. I told her about me and Karl going steady.

Hannah: "I wonder what's it like to go steady."

Me: "Well, this dance was the first time we actually got to go somewhere. Karl mostly just comes by our place with his Dad. We talk. I watch him blow smoke rings. We're like friends, I guess."

Hannah: "His sister's getting married in June."

Me: "I know."

Hannah: "So, do you guys ever talk about the wedding?"

Me: "Of course."

Hannah: "You'll probably marry Karl someday."

Me: "No way."

I saw Karl once more at church on Sunday morning, before Hannah and the Slocumbs brought me home. Afterward he came up to me. I asked him if he had fun at the dance.

Karl: "Well, what do you think?"

Me: "I asked you first."

Karl: "I think you know the answer."

That was all he said. But he winked at me and went off with a bunch of other skinheads. Probably to smoke cigarettes.

Anyway, I tried to tell Hannah about you. "I've been writing letters to my new pen pal. But I don't have any way to send them."

Instead of offering to mail them, she asked me all sorts of questions like, "What's her name? Where's she from?"

I clammed up and chickened out. Sorry. Even Hannah can be a gossip sometimes. So I have to be careful what I say. I'm afraid she'll tell her mom, and her mom will tell Shelly. And Shelly will tell Daddy.

It's what he said about Florida that makes me nervous. He said it was an evil place. He probably means the divorce. The trouble is, I don't remember the bad stuff. All I remember is my mommy. And he never says what it was all about. I just know if he finds out I'm still writing to you, he'll put a stop to it.

I don't think I should tell him about going steady with Karl either. What if he gets mad and says Karl can't come by here with his dad anymore? It's not exactly like I get to go anywhere anyway. I don't even know whether I love Karl or not. I've never thought about him that way. Does he love me? He never actually said it. If I learned nothing else from Mommy and Daddy's divorce, I know I must have love with marriage.

Anyway, I'm really sorry I didn't get your letters mailed this time. Please forgive me. I promise I'll keep working on it.

Your friend,

Sarah

Monday, November 4

Dear Juniper,

Shelly's really getting on my nerves!

At the dance on Saturday, I accidentally dropped a speck of caramel on the collar of her white silk blouse I borrowed. It wasn't any big deal. Mrs. Slocumb helped me treat the stain with baking soda and dish soap. Then I hand washed it.

While Hannah and Mrs. Slocumb were still here yesterday, I made a special point of returning it to Shelly, all washed and ironed. Mrs. Slocumb showed her how we got most of the stain out. There was just a tiny, little, pale yellow spot in the seam, on the corner of the collar. Shelly was gracious about it in front of them.

Then today, out of the blue, she filled a pail with hot water and Clorox bleach, shoved a scrub brush in my hand and said, "As penance for spoiling my best blouse, you can go and clean the outhouse."

Me: "But I spent all last month scrubbing that dang outhouse, just so I could sleep over at Hannah's. It's the boys' turn this week. Daddy even said so."

Shelly: "Well now, your daddy's nowhere around, is he?"

It was true. Daddy headed down to the Camp after lunch. He was planning to go to the meeting of the Order tonight. Mr. Slocumb made a point yesterday of asking him to come, especially.

Anyway, Shelly had me cornered. So I just flat out refused to clean the dang outhouse. And banished my own self to the loft.

Then she followed me up the ladder and threw her white silk blouse in my face. "Here! Use this to clean with. You're the one who ruined it."

Me: "I never did! I said I was sorry about the stain. Look. You can't even see it. You said so yourself."

Shelly: "Well I looked at it again, in the sunlight. And it's ruined, I tell you. Now pick your penance. It's either go clean the outhouse, or do the dishes for the rest of the week."

Me: "I'm telling Daddy about this tomorrow. I did my penance when I washed and ironed your blouse. He won't like you making something more of it, like this."

Shelly: "You best keep your trap shut, little girl. Or I'll tell your daddy on you for going steady with Karl Fisher. He'll definitely make something more of that."

Me: "All right then, dishes it is. Now leave me alone."

Can you believe this? Hannah Slocumb is such a blabbermouth! Now Shelly has something to hold over my head. Hannah must've told her mom about me and Karl going steady. And her mom probably blabbed it to Shelly yesterday, when I wasn't looking.

Anyway, I can't stop thinking about something Hannah told me. We were eating homemade pickles and bread twists in Slocumbs' kitchen during the middle of the night.

I said, "I can't believe all the people at the dance who came up and talked to my daddy. He's like, famous or something."

Hannah: "That's all Shelly's doing. She told my mom all about the feds wanting your daddy to rat on the Order. Now everybody knows."

Boy, when Shelly and Mrs. Slocumb get together they must blab about everything! Like the Camp gossips or something. Daddy specifically ordered Shelly to keep her big mouth shut. I'm sure he doesn't know anything about this. And if he ever finds out, she'll be in a whole heap of trouble.

The problem for me is whether I should use what I know to get out of a week's worth of scrubbing pots and pans. Or should I bide my time, and wait for a bigger bombshell. Knowing Daddy, he will not approve of her gossiping. He's a man of his word. I believe he meant what he said about keeping the visit from the feds to ourselves.

To tell you the truth, I don't think Daddy always trusts some of the men in the Order. Like Mr. Champion. But I never said anything about anything to Hannah. Thanks to Shelly, too much has been said already.

For the time being, I have to be satisfied that I have something to hang over Shelly's head. When the time is right I'll use it to my advantage. I guess I'd better sign off before she catches me with these letters and winds up with something else over my head.

All of a sudden my life seems super complicated. At least I have you to talk to. I know I can trust you.

Good night Juniper. Wherever you are.

Your friend,

Sarah

Friday, November 15

Dear Juniper,

I was lying here on my bed staring at the candle glow, thinking about the night Karl kissed me. It was my first kiss. When I closed my eyes I could feel the way his lips touched my lips. It tingled. Honest. My heart was thumping in my ears. I remember I could hardly breathe.

Did you know when a boy gets that close, you can actually smell him? Karl smelled like sweet smoke. Sweet from eating too many popcorn balls, and smoke from too many cigarettes. I still don't know whether I love him. But I do love the way it felt when he kissed me. I'm not sure if that's a sin. And I guess I'd rather not find out just yet.

Anyway, Karl and Mr. Fisher came by today. He was all business as usual. I just can't figure him out. Even though it's getting pretty cold outside, I stood behind the garage and watched him smoke his cigarette.

Karl: "Couple feds in a black Jeep passed by us on the way up here. They come by to get some more information?"

61

Me: "No!"

Karl: "Your daddy make up his mind whether to rat on the Order?"

Me: "I told you that was a big, fat lie."

I knew it wasn't, but I didn't want to get caught up in the same trap as Shelly.

Karl (grabbing me by the arm): "Things been going pretty good for you folks these days. Your daddy working for the government now?"

"Karl Fisher! That's the dumbest thing you ever said to me." I stomped on his steel-toed combat boot and shook my arm free. Then I really let him have it, both barrels. "How do you think I feel? Stuck up here on this mountain! I hardly ever get to see my friends. Daddy won't even let us go to church anymore."

Karl: "Ain't it enough that I come up and see you? Or are you wanting to see other guys. Like Mitchell Farmer."

Me: "Mitchell Farmer!"

Karl: "I seen you talking to him at the dance."

Me: "He was just asking after my daddy. That's all."

Karl: "You all stopped by his house before you left town that Sunday."

Me: "His Mom had some clothes for the boys. That's all. Karl Fisher! Are you jealous?"

Karl: "Not. Just getting the story straight. Farmer said something totally different."

Me: "Like what."

Karl: "Never mind. I'll set that Nazi straight when I get back to Camp. You're my girl."

Then he snorted and spit out a huge wad. Ugh. I don't know. When he talks like that, I feel like I'm not anybody's girl. I can only guess what Mitchell Farmer told him. What is it with guys? Why do I have to belong to somebody?

I don't know if you have a boyfriend yet, Juniper. But if you do, I hope he's not as much trouble as Karl. When he acts like he did today, I just don't see how I could ever really love him. I don't mind if the man I love is unpredictable. But Karl can be downright mean.

I'm going super crazy up on this mountain. I just want to be free and have fun. Is that too much to ask?

Shelly and Daddy keep forgetting to buy cat food when they go out for supplies. Poor Ginny hasn't had much of anything but mice and macaroni. I'm not supposed to, but I've started saving some of my supper and feeding her at night when I go to bed. It serves two purposes. Fills her tummy and also keeps her busy while I write letters to you. I've been having an awful time lately with her grabbing my pencil when I'm writing. She loves the candlelight. But it makes her wacky, I'm telling you. She already finished eating the venison burger and macaroni casserole I gave her. Then she cleaned herself and curled up to sleep. Makes me sleepy just watching her.

Good night Juniper. Wherever you are.

Your friend,

Sarah

Thursday, November 28

Dear Juniper,

Normally I would wish you a Happy Thanksgiving. But this is not a happy day for me. I'm horribly depressed. Here it is Thanksgiving Day and I've been locked out here in the birthing shed. If it wasn't for Ginny the cat, I'd be all by myself.

Everyone else has gone to the Thanksgiving celebration down at the Camp. Every year they have a turkey shoot and a huge potluck dinner. Before they left, Shelly brought out a big pot of bean soup, a loaf of bread, and a jug of water for the prisoner. Namely me.

It all started yesterday when I got my first menstrual period. I didn't want to tell Shelly, because of the birthing shed.

Whenever Shelly gets her period, Daddy makes her stay out in this birthing shed all by herself. He says according to the Bible, women are unclean during their time of the month. It is penance for Eve's original sin. Shelly (and now me) has to stay out here until she's washed herself clean again. She even stayed here during labor and delivery, when Joseph was born.

65

Hannah told me they don't have a birthing shed at her house. In fact, once I heard Mrs. Slocumb tell Shelly she'd never even heard of such a thing.

But Daddy says, "It's Yashua's law. The Bible says, how can he be clean that is born of woman."

When I stayed over at Hannah's, I confided in her how much I dreaded my first menstrual period because of the birthing shed. She gave me a box of Kotex pads, which I smuggled home in my overnight bag, then hid them under my bed.

But yesterday Shelly walked in on me in the outhouse and caught me changing pads.

I begged. I pleaded. I cried. I screamed.

"Please. Please. Please. Please! Don't make me go to the birthing shed. Not at Thanksgiving!"

Shelly: "We'll see what your daddy says."

Me: "Please don't tell Daddy! He'll make me go. You know he'll make me go! I'll even share my box of pads with you. Then neither one of us will have to stay out there. Please!"

Shelly: "What's with you and that birthing shed? It just so happens I like it out there. For me it's a time of prayer. Peace and quiet. You'll get used to it."

Me: "But I don't want to get used to it. I'll die if you make me stay out there!"

Anyway, she wasn't fooling me. She didn't like the birthing shed because of the peace and quiet. She just liked getting out of days and days of hard work around here.

Shelly: "Don't think for one minute your daddy's not gonna hear about this. If you don't tell him yourself, then I will. And you know very well, if you don't do as you're told, it'll go much worse for you."

Well Juniper, I really let her have it. Both barrels. I lost control.

Me: "It just so happens I know all about what you've been up to. If you tell Daddy about this, I'll tell him that you've been gossiping to Mrs. Slocumb. I'll tell him everybody knows about the feds coming here and asking him to get them information."

For one second she looked shocked. Then she snapped back at me, "Won't do you no good. Your Daddy knows all about what everybody's saying. After all, he was at the dance, too. And he knows it wasn't me talking. It was everybody else."

Me: "Ha! You're bluffing. He hates gossip. He'd be furious if he knew."

Shelly: "If you say one word, I'll be sure and tell him you're going steady with Karl Fisher. Not to mention smoking behind the garage."

Me: "That's not true! I don't smoke."

Shelly: "You heard what I said. Better keep your mouth shut."

Of course I did. Without Hannah here to back me up with her story about Shelly's gossiping, I didn't see how I had any other choice. I knew what a big deal Shelly could make about me and Karl. I couldn't risk it. I need my friends too much right now.

Doomed by my fate, I went and told Daddy about my menstrual period and he sent me to the birthing shed. So here I sit. This place is so cold and damp. Thank heaven for Ginny. So far she's killed three mice and about a dozen spiders. I'd go stark raving mad without her. It smells super gross in here. Like a big, old stinky outhouse. Shelly gave me some incense to burn. But it stinks even worse and gives me a headache. Anyway, I hate her. She did this to me.

Now that I think about it I don't remember anybody at the Harvest Dance saying anything to daddy about being an informant. Or working for the feds. Shelly's all wrong. He thinks the gossip is about the warrant. I'm certain he doesn't know what Shelly's done.

Oh Juniper, why didn't I stick to my guns? I should've told Daddy about her gossiping. I don't even care if she tells him about Karl and me. I hate this place! You can't imagine what it's like. I have to wear my nightgown and lay on this crummy, old cot and bleed onto a towel. It's up to me to wash it out and hang it over the stove to dry, then I start all over with another towel. It's so yucky and embarrassing. I don't even want to talk about it anymore.

I've never been so bored. The batteries ran out in my boom box this morning. I guess I fell asleep with the radio on last night.

Besides reading books, I've been thinking about Florida. Trying to remember Thanksgiving back then. But I can't remember much about it. I know there was a holiday where we drove in the car to see Grandma and Grandpa. Then we ate a huge turkey dinner. But nothing else stands out about it in my mind.

It feels like it might have been a sad time. Like something bad happened. Maybe Mommy and Daddy got the divorce around Thanksgiving. I'm not sure. The only way to describe the feeling is creepy. Like Halloween should feel, and doesn't.

This is turning out to be a long day. Everyone else will be back home tonight. I can't believe I'm missing all that fun down at the Camp.

Before she left, I warned Shelly that she better not blab to everyone about what happened to me. "Just tell them I'm sick with the flu."

I hope and pray she keeps her big mouth shut. It's just too embarrassing to think about Karl and everyone else knowing why I'm locked out here in this shed on Thanksgiving. I don't even want to think about it.

At least I'm not too embarrassed to talk to you about this.

I know you understand. Of course I'll continue to write, in hopes of sending these letters one day. After all, you are my only real contact with the outside world. Wherever you are.

Your friend,

Sarah

Monday, December 9

Dear Juniper,

Pardon my anger, but I'm so riled up right now I have to get this off my chest.

Hannah and the Slocumbs came by today. Daddy and Mr. Slocumb headed off to some secret meeting place for the Order. I guess Karl was right about spotting the feds out on the road. Evidently they really are out there spying on everybody. It just means the members will have to be more careful where they hold their meetings from now on.

Then of all things, Shelly took off with Mrs. Slocumb to go shopping at the Christmas Craft Bazaar in Sandpoint. They left me and Hannah here to babysit Millie and the boys. Can you believe it?

Before Shelly left, I cornered her in the kitchen and let her have it.

Me: "How am I supposed to do my Christmas shopping?"

Shelly: "Well you've got more time than money. I suggest you get creative and make your own gifts this year."

Me: "This is so unfair! Me and the boys are like prisoners here. You and Daddy get to go wherever you want."

Shelly: "Some day you'll be a grown up and you can make your own rules. For now, you're still a kid and you have to do what your daddy says."

Me: "The least you can do is bring back some cat food for poor Ginny. And get me some more books to read. I can't even get to the library anymore."

I must've made her feel guilty because she brought home a bag of cat chow and two books. *Katie John* and *Depend on Katie John*.

Katie John is such a goody-goody. Is she trying to tell me something?

Then she taunted me with, "There was a great used book sale going on at the craft bazaar."

She knows how much I love book sales. Well, I'll fix her. She's not getting any present from me this year. So there!

Hannah brought over three books from the Babysitters Club. It's a series. I've never read any of them. Babysitting's all I ever do anyway. Maybe I should write my own book.

As if things weren't bad enough already, Hannah told me she saw Karl at the Turkey Shoot Ball on Thanksgiving. "He was dancing with Elizabeth Champion."

Who just so happens to be the daughter of the Grand Master himself. And she's 14, no less.

Me: "So I guess he's found a new girlfriend."

Hannah: "Are you mad at him?"

Me: "I don't know. Maybe I'm not enough of a Nazi for him. Anyway, how can I blame him? It's kind of hard to go steady when I never even get to go anywhere."

Hannah: "I know. I heard about what happened to you on Thanksgiving."

Me: "Gees! I can't believe this. I told Shelly to keep her big mouth shut. Does Karl know?"

Hannah shrugged. "If he does, he didn't hear it from me."

Me: "But of course there's always my wicked blabbermouth stepmother."

Hannah tried not to laugh. "What happened to those pads I gave you?"

Me: "Shelly caught me with them."

Hannah: "Do you have enough left for next time?"

I nodded. "She didn't even think to take them away from me."

Hannah: "Gees. What in the world did you do out in the shed all that time?"

I shuddered. "It was horrible. I don't even want to talk about it."

So. Karl was dancing with Elizabeth Champion. Well I can tell you one thing. I'm not going to get all riled up and jump to conclusions like he did over Mitchell Farmer. Maybe he just danced with her. And that's all. The problem is, I wasn't there. He had every right to dance with someone else. Even if she is the Grand Master's daughter.

Anyway, it doesn't look like I'm going to get to the post office any time soon. All I do around here is work. I never have any fun. All I want is to go to town for one lousy day. Is that too much to ask? Sure looks like it. This better not get any worse.

Your friend,

Sarah

Wednesday, December 25

Dear Juniper,

I can't even bring myself to wish you a Merry Christmas. Life just keeps on playing such cruel tricks on me.

Monday I got my menstrual period. Again. I was using the pads and keeping the whole thing hidden. Then yesterday, Christmas eve day, I woke up with terrible cramps. Come to find out, I had bled through a pad onto my nightgown. Shelly caught me furiously trying to rinse it out.

So now I'm back out here in this crummy old shed on Christmas day. While everyone else is over at the house enjoying roast duck, Christmas goodies, and presents. All I have is Ginny to celebrate Christmas with me.

Abraham came out to visit me this afternoon. He brought my presents.

"Take them back!" I yelled at him. "I don't want any stupid presents. Besides nobody's getting anything from me this year."

Abraham: "Not even me?"

He looked like he might start crying. I felt bad. So I told him he could have my rifle. "It's over there by the door. Merry Christmas."

He went over and picked it up eagerly. "But what about you? I know for a fact Daddy didn't get you a new rifle for Christmas."

Me: "I don't want that gun anymore. It's guns that got Daddy in all this trouble with that warrant in the first place."

Abraham shrugged. "Okay by me."

He stayed awhile longer and we played checkers while I sat huddled beneath this scratchy blanket in my nightgown. I was curious, so I asked him if he remembered anything about Christmas in Florida. He shook his head like he couldn't care less and concentrated on his next move.

Me: "Do you remember Mommy?"

He nodded.

Me: "Like, what do you remember most?"

Abraham: "She used to kiss me. Like all the time."

Then he spotted my notebook of letters to you. I'd forgotten to hide it under the blanket when he came in.

Abraham: "You still writing letters to that girl in Florida? I thought Daddy made you burn them. If he catches you, he'll chew your butt."

Me: "Don't you dare tell Daddy. Or I'll take back my gun."

Abraham: "I don't care about your stupid, old letters anyway. Cuz I don't even remember anybody named Juniper. You probably just made it all up."

Me: "I did not. Juniper was my best friend. Just go on. Get out of here. Leave me alone."

When he left, he took the gun but forgot the presents. What a geek. But I didn't open them. I don't know why my brother doesn't remember you. Maybe he was just too little back then. But I do remember. And that's all that matters.

This is the worst Christmas of my entire life. And I've had some bad ones, believe me. Like the time we were living in our camper with Daddy in Michigan. I was eight. The camper was parked in the farmyard of some friends of Daddy's. Two brothers. Daddy stayed up really late on Christmas eve talking politics inside the farmhouse. We didn't even have a Christmas tree.

On Christmas morning he didn't wake up until noon. All we got for presents was socks and underwear and a candy cane. Daddy took us to a place called the Salvation Army where we ate mushy turkey, cold mashed potatoes, and soggy apple pie with a whole bunch of weird looking strangers. It was awful.

At least there was an old man in a Santa suit who gave me and Abraham each a teddy bear. Mine was a black and white panda with a huge red and green bow. I still have it. I call it Juniper. I hope you don't mind. Anyway you can see how this is way worse.

I remember our very last Christmas with my mommy. I got the Barbie condo. Grandma and Grandpa came. They brought tons of presents for everyone. We all went to church and sang Christmas songs. Everyone held lighted candles. It was beautiful.

There's something else I remember about Christmas in Florida. A little boy with blond hair, dressed in a dark red velvet suit with short pants and knee socks. He wore a little candy-cane bow tie. And a Rudolph the red-nosed reindeer pin. The nose actually lit up. The little boy called it his blinky button. By any chance do you have a little brother?

I know it's not Abraham. Because for one thing he doesn't look a bit like him. And for another, Abraham wouldn't be caught dead in anything but bib overalls. Believe me. Anyway, something tells me the little boy's name was Austin. I don't know for sure. Maybe he was just a kid from church.

Daddy showed up with supper just before dark. Leftover duck with mashed potatoes, cole slaw, and the pumpkin pie I baked yesterday. Before they locked me in here.

He brought my rifle back and chewed my butt for giving it away. "Remember, we must arm ourselves to prepare for Armageddon."

Then he noticed the wrapped gifts by the door. "What are your presents doing over there? You haven't opened them."

Me: "I don't want any presents. I didn't give anyone else any presents."

Daddy: "I see. You're mad because you have to spend Christmas in the birthing shed, so you're bringing penance on yourself. Tell me, how does your behavior serve Yashua?"

Me: "All I know is I live like a prisoner. And I never even did anything wrong."

Daddy: "The Bible says, suffer the little children. Better take up your Bible and study hard. Find your strength in Yashua's Word."

And that was that.

I only wish I could find a way to mail these letters. I would so much like to get letters from you all about your beautiful Christmas and all the presents you got. I could really use some good news for a change.

I miss you. Wherever you are.

Your friend,

Sarah

Saturday, January 4

Dear Juniper,

The heavy snows always come to northern Idaho in January. We're having our first blizzard today. So far, it looks like about a foot of snow. But it was still snowing when I went up to bed.

Daddy has a snowplow attachment for his pickup. But the wind was so bad, he couldn't even see to plow the driveway. We'll be snowbound up here until the weather calms down.

Daddy got to go to a meeting of the Order this week before the snow fell. He drove down to Sandpoint on Monday. Mr. Slocumb met him there. He was worried about being followed by the feds. He didn't get home until long after I fell asleep, which is normal for meeting nights. At least he brought home food and supplies.

Karl and Mr. Fisher came by yesterday before the storm. Their visits have become the absolute highlight of my existence. Although I just can't figure out Karl. He got a new 9mm semiautomatic handgun for Christmas. Police issue. Very cool. He brought it along just to show off.

He also brought me Christmas presents. A Garth Brooks cassette, and fresh batteries for my boom box. Sometimes he can be such a sweetheart. The trouble is, all he ever wants to talk about is Daddy's business with the feds and the stupid warrant.

After I thanked him for such nice gifts, I confessed, "I'm really sorry that I don't have a present for you. It's just that me and the boys have been stuck here since the Harvest Dance. But Daddy and Shelly get to go wherever they want."

Karl: "It's for your own good. You're just too young to understand the danger."

Me: "What danger? It doesn't feel like that to me."

Karl: "You don't know what's going on out there. Feds've been spotted all over these mountains. They're spying on your daddy pretty regular. In fact someone could be watching us this very minute."

Me: "Oh stop it! You don't scare me."

Karl: "Well you should be scared. Rumor has it they'd like to get their hands on you kids. And use you to get to your daddy. Turn you against him."

Me: "Ha! That'll never happen in a million years."

Karl: "Don't be too sure. Anything's possible. What I don't get is how come they haven't arrested your daddy by now."

Me: "What do you mean by that? Do you want him to get arrested?"

Karl: "Never said that. Just doesn't add up, is all."

I swear Karl has more opinions than the guy on the radio–Rush Limbaugh.

I guess it's true what he said. The feds could stop Daddy and arrest him at any time. I've pestered Daddy and Shelly relentlessly about taking me to town. He swears he's taking a huge risk every time he leaves the property. But he never said a word about the feds wanting to get hold of us kids.

Of course all Shelly ever says is how much she depends on me to babysit. For her information, my name is not Katie John.

All I want to do is go to the post office. I never dreamed your letters wouldn't get mailed yet. And now a great big, huge stumbling block has come to my attention. So much has been written down here about Karl and Hannah, and even Shelly. Personal things which might offend them. Or worse, embarrass me.

One day when you finally read these letters, you'll understand why, at this point, I've decided to wait out the warrant, then mail them myself. I'm afraid if I hand them over to anyone else, they'll certainly be read by curious eyes. And I could wind up in a heap of trouble.

Well Juniper, my candle is burning out. And our supply is running low. I'd better sign off for now.

Your friend,

Sarah

Tuesday, January 7

Dear Juniper,

Just as I feared, things have taken a turn for the worse. I guess I should've seen it coming. I mean Karl practically warned me himself. Daddy was arrested today. As far as I know, he's still in jail tonight.

After the holidays and the big snow storm, we were running very low on our food and supplies. So Daddy and Shelly left for town late this morning. Again I was stuck at home, babysitting the boys. But for once it turned out to be lucky for me.

As you might have guessed we're down to eggs, eggs, and more eggs. I used up the last of the mayonnaise making egg-salad sandwiches for lunch. I expected Daddy and Shelly back before supper so I didn't plan to fix anything. When they didn't come home I made omelets. All I could find to put in them was canned tuna.

"This is gross!" Abraham protested the meal. He was right.

Me: "I know. Sorry. It was all I could find for us to eat."

Abraham: "Where's Daddy and Shelly anyway? Why aren't they back yet?"

Me: "I don't know. Maybe they had a flat tire or something."

I kind of pretended it wasn't any big deal. Except I knew very well when they hadn't come home by supper time, something must be wrong. Naturally I couldn't get the boys to go to bed. They insisted on waiting up.

It was long after dark by the time Shelly walked through the door all by herself. She was pretty riled up.

Immediately I asked, "Where's Daddy?"

She looked awful tired. "It's a long story. And I need a cup of tea."

I jumped up. "I'll make some."

Shelly: "Is there anything to eat around here? I'm starving."

"Yeah. Eggs!" I stared at her. "Aren't there any groceries out in the truck?"

Much to my dismay she shook her head. "We never made it to Sam's Club."

While I fixed her tea and a fried egg sandwich, she told us what happened. "This morning we got as far as Meadow Creek. We saw what we thought was an old couple looking under the hood of their pickup camper. Looked like it had stalled on the bridge. Your daddy got out to see if he could help. All of a sudden it seemed like feds came out of nowhere, armed to the teeth. Two of them ran out of the woods in front of the camper. They drew their weapons and threw your daddy to the ground. Two more jumped out of the back of the camper in front of me and pulled me out of the pickup."

At that point, Abraham got pretty excited. He grabbed his gun and aimed it at the door. "Shoulda shot 'em dead right then."

Me: "Don't be silly. They were outnumbered. They could've been killed!"

"That's right! Besides, I didn't have a chance. They threw me down on the ground, too. Look at my arms! They're all scratched up." Shelly showed us her arms. Sure enough, they looked scraped and bruised from the scuffle.

Me: "Did they arrest you?"

"Well, they took both of us down to Sandpoint. They arrested your daddy and put him in jail. They questioned me for hours. But I refused to tell them anything. So finally they gave me the keys to the truck and sent me home. Alone."

Me: "What's going to happen to Daddy?"

She wiped tears from her eyes. "I don't know. They said he has to go before the magistrate in court tomorrow morning."

Me: "Are you going to go back there?"

Shelly: "Of course. I have to find out whatever information I can. Maybe they'll let him go. At the very least, I need to make another attempt to get to Sam's Club."

"Before we all die from an overdose of eggs," I muttered.

Abraham: "Can we go with you?"

Shelly: "No. It's much too dangerous. Your daddy expects you boys to keep the fires burning in the stoves. So we don't all freeze to death. And Sarah, I need you to stay here with them."

I shuddered. After all that, you can imagine how disappointed I feel. It seems so unfair. But I guess Daddy would want me to stay here. And Shelly's right about supplies. She has to try again. We're down to rationing everything. I shouldn't even be using my last candle to write to you.

All our batteries are dead. No boom box. No clock. I don't even know what time it is anymore. Luckily the moon is waxing full this week, so we're not in total darkness in the mad dash to pee.

I wonder how long they'll keep my daddy in jail. I can't imagine how we can get along without him. Guess I'd better say my prayers extra long tonight.

Your friend,

Sarah

Wednesday, January 8

Dear Juniper,

It was bitter cold this morning. Ten degrees. With a wind chill to boot. At least we have plenty of firewood for the stoves. Shelly got up before sunrise and drove to Sandpoint for the court thing.

I made pancakes for breakfast. We were out of everything to put on them: maple syrup, butter, honey, and peanut butter. All I could find was a jar of tahini, which is sesame-seed butter. Looks like baby poop. Tastes like soggy pie crust. Disgusting. But I just couldn't bring myself to fix more eggs. I've eaten so many eggs this week they're coming out of my ears. Scrambled eggs. Poached eggs. Fried eggs. Hard-boiled eggs. Creamed eggs. Omelets. Pancakes. Custard. Ugh.

We bake our own bread. So there's plenty of it. For lunch I gave the boys their choice between bread and tahini, or eggs. To my complete amazement, they all asked for fried egg sandwiches. I don't know anymore which is worse, eggs or tahini. Luckily,

Daddy and Shelly arrived home soon after and rescued us from this scrambled-egg hell.

Thank heavens they'd managed to get to Sam's Club after Daddy got out of jail. He looked real tired. Since he was way behind on his chores from being gone overnight, he high-tailed it outdoors right away to catch up. I figured whenever he was ready, he'd tell us kids what happened today. I was just relieved to have him back home.

Abraham shot a snowshoe hare from the back porch this afternoon. He was so excited. But Shelly chewed his butt for shooting off his gun so close to the house. She said Travis or Joseph could've come around the corner and accidentally stepped into his rifle sight. Even though I know she's right, I felt sorry for my brother. He tried to make up for his blunder by totally skinning and cleaning the rabbit by himself. Shelly cooked it in a casserole called Hasenpfeffer. Adding insult to injury, the meat was tough and stringy. But the onion gravy and noodles were tasty. Beats eggs!

All Daddy said was, "Shot him on the run, didn't you, son?"

Poor Abraham. He was just trying to help.

After supper, Daddy explained the situation to us. "I told the magistrate in court today that I am not guilty of those charges against me. And that it's my intention to go to trial. Then he told me if this case goes to trial and I lose, the government could very well take away my home and property."

Me: "How can they do that?"

"The feds can do anything they want. The Bible says the beast will try to take your soul. All the more reason for us to stand and fight. On our way to Armageddon." Then he read from the Bible, Revelation 2:10. "Fear none of those things which thou shalt suffer; behold, the devil shall cast some of you into prison, that ye may be tried; and ye shall have tribulation ten days: be thou faithful unto death, and I will give thee a crown of life."

Then we all joined hands and prayed to Yashua for guidance. I battled the tears in my eyes. There's been more than enough trouble these past few days. I'm exhausted.

Your friend,

Sarah

Friday, January 17

Dear Juniper,

Karl and Mr. Fisher showed up here today. I wasn't exactly surprised to see them. Mr. Fisher surprised us with a tray from the post office. It was overflowing with months and months worth of mail.

Me and Shelly baked raisin and cinnamon coffee cake. I don't know why we couldn't make it with cinnamon and nuts, instead of raisins.

But when I suggested adding nuts, Shelly said, "Good idea. We'll use both."

I swear she puts raisins in everything. Meanwhile the men sat around the table drinking coffee and talking. Daddy sent the boys up to the loft. I felt privileged to stay in the kitchen and listen in on their conversation.

Mr. Fisher explained that Mrs. Beekman, the Bonners Ferry postmaster, asked him to deliver our mail to us. "No doubt she heard about your arrest, Dalton. Said there were some official looking letters in your pile of mail. Frankly, I think the feds got her all worried that she might be held responsible if she didn't see to it that your mail got delivered somehow."

While Mr. Fisher talked, Daddy was digging through the assortment of mail in the cardboard tray. He pulled out one envelope and said, "Either that or they specifically told her to make sure I get my hands on this. Postmarked this week."

He tore it open and read aloud. It was from an officer of the court, named Mr. Sanford. All he said was Daddy's court date was changed from February to March.

Mr. Fisher: "Well that'll give the lawyer more time to work on your case."

Daddy: "Like I said before, no lawyers."

Mr. Fisher: "I don't see how you can expect to win this case without legal help."

Shelly: "He's right, Dalton. They've threatened to take away our home."

Mr. Fisher: "What?!"

Shelly explained how the court magistrate warned them that the government could take his property if Daddy loses at the trial.

Mr. Fisher: "They can't do that! Any lawyer'll tell you that, Dalton. I don't see how you can refuse legal advice with so much at stake."

Daddy: "You know I can't afford that. Besides, I still mean to handle this thing quietly. No publicity. And that's not how lawyers operate."

I caught Mr. Fisher and Karl exchanging glances. Then Mr. Fisher spoke up again. "Guess this is as good a time as any to spill the beans. The members of the Order got together and pooled our resources. With that and the monies from the legal defense fund they started at the Camp last fall, we took the liberty of hiring a lawyer for you."

Daddy: "You expect me to be grateful? The way I see this is you just dug a deeper hole for me. On top of everything else, now I'm beholding to the Order."

Mr. Fisher: "The Order is already beholding to you and your family for taking such a strong stand against the government. You're a hero, Dalton."

Shelly walked over and stood proudly behind Daddy, hands on his shoulders.

Daddy: "Hero's a sandwich. I'm just a gunsmith minding my own business. Leave it alone."

Mr. Fisher: "I'm afraid it's too late for that."

After we finished our warm coffee cake, Karl asked me to go for a walk with him. Of course I knew he just wanted to smoke a cigarette. Instead of going out behind the garage he headed for the back of the chicken coop and lit one up.

Me: "What're we doing over here?"

Karl: "Smoking a cigarette."

Me: "I can see that."

Karl looked suspiciously at the woods surrounding the property.

Me: "What's going on with you?"

Karl: "When are you going to get it? The feds are spying on this place."

Me: "So you said. But it just so happens, I live here. And the only other people I've seen around here is you Fishers and the Slocumbs. I really think you're taking this skinhead thing a bit too far."

Karl: "Think what you want. I happen to know it for a fact."

Me: "So what! I don't have anything to hide."

Karl: "Don't be too sure."

Me: "Oh stop it. You think you're so cool."

He exhaled smoke with the steam from his breath. "I don't think. I am cool." He was really irritating me. So I started to walk away. But he grabbed the sleeve of my jacket. "Your Daddy's none too happy about the lawyer we hired."

I shrugged. "Maybe once he gets used to the idea, he'll think better of it. It's hard to know what's the right thing to do."

Karl: "The Order has to protect themselves too, you know. It's not just about your daddy anymore."

Me: "What do you mean by that?"

Karl: "Some of the members are wondering why the feds released your daddy when he never posted any bail."

Me: "Maybe they figured out he doesn't have any money."

Karl: "Or maybe he struck up some kind of deal with them."

Me: "He did not! How can you say such a thing? Daddy would never make any deals with the feds. He says they're the enemy."

Karl: "Well, enemy or not, right after court your daddy and Shelly were spotted at Sam's Club buying a whole cart full of stuff."

I stomped my feet in frustration and cried out, "For heaven's sake! We were starving. They hadn't been to town in weeks. A harmless trip to Sam's Club. What's that?"

Karl: "Didn't look that way to some folks."

"So now *who's* spying on *who?*" I marched off and left him standing there with the chickens. Dumb cluck.

Oh Juniper, what should I do? I don't know why Karl says such mean, nasty things. I'm positive Daddy didn't make any deals with the feds. And I think I should tell him what Karl said. But I'm afraid if I do, he'll get all riled up. Worst of all, he'd get mad at me for gossiping with Karl about family business. He might not let him come by anymore. And he might even get mad enough at the members of the Order so he won't accept their help. No matter what their intentions are, it does seem like he needs a lawyer. He can't let the government take his home.

Anyway, how can I be sure Karl is even telling the truth? I'm sure you can see the problem. I'm so confused. Perhaps if I pray and then sleep on it, the answer will come to me tomorrow.

Your friend,

Sarah

Friday, January 24

Dear Juniper,

Well, me and Ginny are back in this crummy old birthing shed again. She doesn't mind staying here half as much as I do. I'm grateful for her company. At least I can write my letters to you out here and not worry about getting caught.

It's been a week of hard work around this place. The boys were starting to complain about it last night at supper. I never said a word. It's been a relief to have the sameness of daily chores after so much trouble.

During Bible study, Daddy read from Proverbs 13:4. "The soul of the sluggard desireth, and hath nothing: but the soul of the diligent shall be made fat." Then he added, "Nose to the grindstone, boys. Hard work is the best remedy for your troubles."

If that's true then I'd rather be out there doing chores, than stuck in here worrying about my troubles. And those troubles are certainly piling up around me.

This morning my menstrual period came back. After lunch Shelly stopped me on my way to the outhouse. She found the pad hidden in my pocket. I don't seem to be able to get the hang of keeping this from her.

Anyway, right then Karl and Mr. Fisher drove up.

I panicked and begged her, "Please! Don't make me go to the shed. Not in front of them!"

She caved in. "All right. Just this once. But mark my word young lady, you'll be spending the night out there."

And so I am.

Mr. Fisher brought a newspaper article for Daddy to read. It was from the *Kootenai Valley News*. The article was all about Daddy's arrest and the upcoming trial. Which of course proves he really is famous.

In the article an officer of the court denied that the court date was changed from February to March. He said there was never any letter sent to Dalton Smith.

Well Daddy was furious! I don't remember ever seeing him so riled up.

He waved the newspaper at Mr. Fisher and shouted, "Those filthy liars. I have the letter right here. What're they trying to pull?"

Shelly tried to calm him down. But he would have no part of it and pushed her away.

Mr. Fisher: "Looks like they're just trying to come off hard-nosed to the press."

Daddy: "If they lie to the press so easily, they're probably lying to me. I sure as hell can't trust those feds."

A little while later out behind the chicken coop, Karl said to me, "I don't get why your daddy's so riled up over that newspaper article. He's a celebrity now for sure."

Me: "Daddy doesn't much like publicity. It's not his way."

Karl: "Maybe he's got something to hide."

Me: "If you're just going to stand here, puffing on your coffin nails and bad-mouth my daddy, I'm going back in the house."

Karl: "I never bad-mouthed your daddy. I'm just trying to understand something."

Me: "Understand what?"

Karl: "What is it that he thinks the feds are lying to him about?"

Me: "I don't know. What difference does it make? They sure did lie about that letter he got. My daddy doesn't believe in dealing with liars and thieves."

Karl: "Neither does the Order."

Me: "Then why are they so suspicious of him?"

Karl: "Not everyone. Just a few."

I decided right then and there to take matters into my own hands and give him my very own best assurance. "Well I can swear on a stack of Bibles that Daddy isn't working for the feds."

Karl: "He might not be. But neither you or I can swear that behind closed doors he didn't plea bargain with some information on the Order."

Me: "I've heard just about enough of your skinhead talk! If you really don't trust my daddy, then I don't see how we can continue to go steady. It just wouldn't be right."

Karl: "Sarah, I never said I didn't trust your daddy. I'm only telling you there are certain people out there who don't. This is a warning, you silly girl."

Me: "Why tell me? What am I supposed to do about it?"

Karl: "Pass it on."

Me: "He'll just get all mad at me for gossiping."

Karl: "At least he'll know. We all have to make sacrifices for the cause."

Me: "Then why don't you tell him yourself?"

Karl: "That would make me a traitor to the Order."

Me: "And why aren't you a traitor when you tell me?"

Karl: "Because you're my girl."

Then he surprised me with a kiss. Just one. I didn't dare risk getting caught.

So once more I don't know what to do. If Karl's right, then how do I tell Daddy? It's easy for Karl to talk about sacrifice. He's not the one who has to face up to my daddy with this ugly rumor. I saw how furious he was today when he read that newspaper article. And this news is a whole lot worse.

Anyway, thank heavens I have you to write these letters to. Although I wish I'd been able to mail them months ago. I long to hear from you. To know you're out there, thinking of me. Praying for me.

Sometimes I pretend what it would be like if we could actually meet again. You probably wouldn't recognize me. Nor would I recognize you, I suppose. But I'm quite sure we'd fast become best friends again. Anyway I finally feel sleepy now. Maybe I can get some rest from all this worrying.

Good night Juniper. Wherever you are.

Your friend,

Sarah

Saturday, January 25

Dear Juniper,

As you might've guessed, I'm still in the shed.

Tonight Shelly brought my typewriter out here for me. She wrote a letter and she wants me to type it for her.

Not only was I grateful to have my typewriter and something worthwhile to keep me busy, but I am also very proud that Shelly would give me such an important task. Aside from the fact she can't type, she proved how much she and Daddy really trust me. For this one time, they have allowed me into their grown-ups circle.

Two ideas come to mind. First, I should offer to mail the typed letter so I can finally get the chance to go to the post office and mail your letters. Next, I might consider confiding in Shelly about Karl's warning. She'll know the best way to tell Daddy.

Anyway, I plan to type up the letter tomorrow during daylight. Tonight I'm going to copy it here for you to read also. Here is what the letter says:

"To the servants of the beast government,

'And judgment is turned away backward, and justice standeth afar off; and truth is fallen in the street and equity cannot enter. Yea, truth faileth; and he that departeth from evil is prey to the beast and Yashua saw it and it displeased Him that there was not judgment.' (Isaiah 59:14-15)

"We, the family of Dalton Smith, have been shown by our savior, Yashua that we are to stay sequestered on this property for our cause.

"Almighty Yashua knows you servants of lawlessness are on the side of the beast government.

"Choose this day whom you will serve. As for me and my house, we will serve Yashua.

"Whether we live or die, we will not obey your beast government.

"Repent, for the kingdom of Yashua is at hand."

Well, this is a very serious letter indeed. I didn't read it first before I copied it. I wonder if the "we" includes him and Shelly? And if no one can leave here, then I wonder how Shelly expects to mail her letter?

And the stuff about "whether we live or die." What does she mean by that? Is she taunting them? Remember how spunky she was the day the feds came here last fall. She could very well get us all killed with her reckless words.

All the more reason I should tell her about Karl's warning. She needs to know there are some people who don't trust Daddy. Perhaps this is a sign from Yashua after all. He has answered my prayer for guidance by pointing me in Shelly's direction. At least now I know what to do.

Your friend,

Sarah

Sunday, January 26

Dear Juniper,

I'm back in my own bed tonight. Shelly and I had a huge fight in the shed. I guess as a way of making amends she let me out early. She said I could use pads for the rest of the spotting days. I should be grateful, but instead I feel like a fool for thinking I'd been included in their grown-ups circle.

When Shelly brought out my lunch today, I had just finished typing her letter.

"It's perfect, Sarah," she praised me. "No mistakes. You did a wonderful job. Your daddy will be so proud of you. He wants each one of us to sign it. So I'll let you be the first."

I signed the letter quickly, then offered, "Can I take it to the post office for you?"

Shelly: "Don't be silly. Didn't you read it? We're sequestered. That means we can't leave here."

Me: "I know what it means. I've been sequestered here for months already. So how do you plan to mail this?"

111

Shelly: "Mr. Fisher will mail it for me. He promised your daddy on Friday that he'd bring our supplies if we decided to go through with this."

Me: "What if he reads it? What if he lets someone else read it? What if he doesn't even mail it? "

Shelly: "Why, Sarah Smith. I am surprised at you. Mr. Fisher has been a good friend to us through this. He's Karl Fisher's father after all."

Me: "Listen. There's something you need to know. Karl warned me on Friday that some of the members of the Order think Daddy made a deal with the feds in order to get out of jail without posting bail money."

Shelly: "Who?"

Me: "He didn't say."

Shelly laughed. "Well, there you go. That's just exactly how rumors start. No names. No facts. Just idle gossip. And shame on you for repeating it."

Me: "But we have to tell Daddy. So he can judge for himself."

Shelly: "Young lady, you will not pass on these vicious rumors to your daddy. You know how he hates gossip. You'll only make him more angry than he already is."

Me: "But he has the right to know!"

Shelly: "Know what? It amounts to nothing."

Me: "Well I don't agree. And if you're serious about giving this letter to Mr. Fisher, then I'll tell Daddy myself."

Shelly: "Don't you dare! If you do, I'll tell him about your steady boyfriend. I'll tell him you and Karl were necking in front of the Slocumbs after the Harvest Dance."

Well, I was tongue-tied. She pulled the rug out from under me once again. Who blabbed? Hannah and Mrs. Slocumb?

I handed her the letter.

She drove her point home one last time. "All that talk is just Karl Fisher's way of trying to impress you because your daddy's in the newspaper. For all I know, you and him were out there necking behind those buildings."

Me: "Just take your stupid old letter and get out of here."

She started to leave then stopped at the door. "If you promise to keep your mouth shut and don't upset your Daddy, I'll let you out of here right now."

I was flabbergasted. "What?"

Shelly: "You heard me. You're just spotting now anyway. Use your pads."

Me: "Okay."

Shelly: "Not one word. Promise me!"

I was cornered like one of Ginny's mice. "Whatever."

Juniper, I had no choice. She offered me freedom for my silence. But I don't know if it was the right thing to do. Now I may never know. This is getting so complicated. I wish Karl Fisher had kept his big Nazi mouth shut.

I need to make a trip to the outhouse now, before I go to sleep.

Good night Juniper. Wherever you are.

Your friend,

Sarah

Friday, February 7

Dear Juniper,

Today was the most embarrassing day of my life. You'll never believe what happened here.

Karl and Mr. Fisher came by today as usual. They brought the lawyer with them. His name is Mr. Jameson. He's from Spokane. So he's not a potato head from Boise. I don't know whether it made any difference to Daddy or not.

He seemed nice enough and he wasn't all dressed up in a suit. Which is a good thing, because Daddy always says he doesn't trust a man just because he's dressed in a suit. Luckily for Mr. Jameson he wore a big old wool sweater and slacks instead. And he had large, intelligent eyes behind his glasses.

Right off the bat Daddy told him, "Let's get one thing straight. You will honor my family's right to privacy. I expect you'll see to it there's no TV people up here sticking cameras in our faces."

Mr. Jameson: "Hm. Yes. I understand."

The grown-ups all sat down around the kitchen table drinking coffee. Karl sat right down there with them like a big shot Nazi.

Shelly had made fresh banana bread this morning. So I hung close by in the kitchen slicing and serving it. What a big mistake! The conversation ended with me right in the middle of it. And yes, Shelly put raisins instead of nuts in her dumb banana bread.

Anyway Mr. Jameson took out a thick file folder and yellow pad, then started right in. "I've spent considerable time on this case already. So we have quite a few things to go over. First of all there's this matter of a letter sent to the FBI from your family."

"That's right. I wrote the letter on everyone's behalf," Shelly said, handing him a copy. "This is it right here."

After he finished reading it he said, "Hm. I see. Well. I'm here to tell you they didn't appreciate your effort at all, Mrs. Smith. In fact they consider this letter to be quite inflammatory. They interpreted it as a veiled threat."

Daddy: "Threat of what?"

Mr. Jameson: "Hm. Well. You see, if someone wanted to, they could interpret these words as a threat of violence against the government."

Daddy: "We'll fight to defend our home and property. That much is true."

Mr. Jameson cleared his throat. "While I respect your right to feel the way you do, as your attorney, I must insist from now on all communication between you and the FBI be handled through my office. Please."

Daddy: "A man has the right to say what he thinks."

Mr. Jameson: "Like I said, Mr. Smith, I respect that. The problem here is the government can use a letter like this against you. They can take phrases out of context to make your words seem more dangerous. For instance they could combine two lines into, 'We the family of Dalton Smith will die. We will not obey.' They could make it sound like you pose a threat to your own family's welfare."

Daddy nodded. "I see what you mean. After reading that newspaper story, I can already see how they twist things around."

Mr. Jameson: "Hm. Well, then please let me handle the communication from here on out."

Shelly: "I guess so. But that was a darn good letter I wrote."

He nodded. He sure was a polite man. I just always had this notion that lawyers were rude and bossy. But he seemed okay. Anyway, I must get on with what he said next. Here comes the really awful part. Shelly told me to make another pot of coffee. I'll never forget that moment.

Suddenly Mr. Jameson said, "The next issue we need to discuss involves Sarah. Where's Sarah?"

Proud and tall, I stepped forward out of the shadows and declared, "I'm Sarah."

Mr. Jameson nodded but didn't smile at me. "Yes. Well. I came across some information from one of my sources that the feds have been working on a plan to kidnap Sarah." He looked at me. "This is critical. Do you spend time alone in one of the sheds out on the property?"

The birthing shed! I was speechless. How could the feds possibly know about that? My face felt red hot with embarrassment. I looked desperately at Shelly and Daddy. But they weren't about to keep my secret. I couldn't face Karl.

Daddy spoke up. "During their monthly time the women must go out to the birthing shed and cleanse their bodies of sin."

Mr. Jameson: "Hm. Well, I'm not familiar with the custom. Is this based on your religious beliefs?"

Daddy: "It's based on Yashua's word. And the teachings of the Bible."

Mr. Jameson: "I see. Well. The feds seem to be well aware of your practice. And they see it as child abuse. Their plan is to get inside this birthing shed, as you called it, and take Sarah out with them. They've seen your boys bringing food out to her. They must think they can use the opportunity to get hold of one or more of your kids."

Daddy pounded on the table. "Dammit! That's just like them!"

Startled by his fist, I looked up. Karl was staring at me, then he looked away. I had no idea what he was thinking. I was mortified.

Daddy: "One by one. They take my business, now my family, then my property."

Mr. Jameson: "Hm. Well, they haven't succeeded. Yet. What you need to do is keep the women and children out of the shed from now on. In fact this proves they're watching you. None of you should venture out onto this property alone. But always in pairs, preferably with an adult nearby. Does that make sense to you?"

Daddy nodded. "Of course. They've made us prisoners on our own property in their dirty little war."

Mr. Jameson stood up. "Well. The most important thing is to protect the safety and well-being of your wife and children. Correct?"

Daddy stood up, too. "They will stand and fight alongside me. That is Yashua's law."

Mr. Jameson: "Hm. Yes. Well, let's see to it the fight you speak of is in a court of law and not a bloody battleground."

Shelly piped up. "First they set him up. Then they spy on us. Now they make out like he's threatening the government. I don't see how Dalton can even expect a fair trial."

Mr. Jameson: "Hm. Well, it's my job to see that he does."

Daddy shook his hand. "So be it then. Yashua's will be done."

Karl motioned for me to go out for a walk with him before they left, but I couldn't even look him in the eye, much less talk to him. I fled to the loft instead. I've never been so embarrassed. So exposed. Think of it. On the one hand, this means I don't have to go out to that stinking shed anymore, which is glorious news. On the other hand, now everybody knows about it. Think of the gossip! I thought I'd die right there in front of Karl.

After Mr. Jameson and the Fishers left, Daddy told Shelly she was right. "The feds wanted an informant. So they tricked me with that gun deal. When I wouldn't cooperate, they arrested me. Now they're spying on us. Hell, they're trying to steal my kids! If the feds can make a humble man like me out to be a threat to their beast government, then I've seen just about everything."

Shelly: "I'm afraid the best we can hope for is that the lawyer will get those charges dropped."

Daddy: "You know as well as I do that's not gonna happen. The feds've got it in for me. There's no justice in their courts. I can tell you that much."

Anyway, I can't stop thinking about the whole thing with the FBI planning to kidnap me. Talk about scary. I had no idea the danger was so close. When I think of all the days and nights I spent out there. Alone. Never knowing. It makes me shudder to think what might've happened. I could've been kidnapped by feds. Maybe even killed!

All that's left for me to do is pray Yashua will watch over me. I know if you could, you would pray for me too, Juniper. Wherever you are.

Your friend,
Sarah

Monday, February 10

Dear Juniper,

Ever since the lawyer informed us that our every move is being watched, Daddy has been busy drawing maps and teaching me and the boys how to patrol. It's not exactly hard. We know the trails already.

If he said it once, he's said it a thousand times. "The three of you keep together. And take Yeller along." We spent most of Saturday and Sunday traipsing after him along the property lines. "Always remember to carry your rifles."

Otherwise I've been keeping pretty much to myself since the whole embarrassing scene in front of the lawyer and everyone.

Abraham was the most talkative out on the trail. "What're we supposed to be looking for?"

Daddy: "Anything and everything. Intruders. Booby traps. Footprints. Campsites. Tree stands. Any sign that someone's been out here."

Travis ran ahead of us and plucked a shell casing out of the dirt.

"Good job, son," Daddy said, praising him. "Shell casing. There's your proof right there. Someone's definitely been out here."

Abraham: "But I never heard any gunshots."

Daddy: "That's why we're out here. You can't see what you're not looking for. And you can't hear what you're not listening to. A single rifle shot could easily get past our ears unnoticed. Now that we've seen this shell casing, we all know what to listen for. Next time those cowards come sneaking around here and fire a single shot in the air like a signal, you can rest assured more than one of us will hear it."

Abraham: "What happens if we actually see somebody?"

Daddy: "Order them to leave the property. If they refuse, stand your ground. Fire a warning shot in the air. Help will come."

Anyway, today I went out with Travis and Abraham on our first patrol without Daddy. We took Yeller with us of course, and our rifles. We hiked the trails on the north side of the property, which is toward the national forest. Daddy wanted us to check and see if the feds had set up any campsites. But we didn't see anything.

The hardest part was keeping those boys together. They were real jittery. Even the crackling of a twig in the woods got them all riled up, until they realized it was only a squirrel. By then the trail was getting pretty muddy so we turned back. Tomorrow we patrol the west trail. I just hope those boys settle down once they learn the routine. They don't listen to me.

Well Juniper, Shelly's waiting for me to go to the outhouse with her. It's part of the new security plan. As if we weren't already prisoners here. Now we can't even enjoy normal privacy for the simplest things.

I wonder how long we'll have to live like this. I pray Yashua will release the Smith family from these chains.

Your friend,

Sarah

Friday, February 14

Dear Juniper,

Happy Valentine's Day!

What a crazy, mixed-up day this has been! Can you believe it? I forgot all about it until today. I even wrote an essay for the history lesson called, "Young Abe Lincoln" on his birthday. But I still forgot Valentine's Day.

Of course this is one of those pagan holidays like Halloween that Daddy doesn't allow us to celebrate. On top of everything else going on around here, it's no wonder I forgot.

Karl and Mr. Fisher came by today. I wish I would've at least remembered to make a valentine for Karl. Especially since it was the first time I've seen him after my most embarrassing moment. I felt doubly awkward.

I tried to avoid him at first by unpacking the groceries they brought. Karl went outside with Daddy and Mr. Fisher to check out our new security measures, like the padlocks on the outbuildings. Plus we started building booby traps at each trail head. I knew Karl would think it was cool.

When I came upon the sack containing a large box of Kotex pads, I made myself nauseous worrying about whether or not he'd seen them. So I dashed outside for some air.

Of course Karl came right over to me on the porch. "You okay? You're all white."

I couldn't look at him. "Yeah. Sure."

"Come with me. I forgot something in the truck." He didn't exactly wait for an answer so I followed him as he got into the front seat . There he handed me a red, heart-shaped box of chocolates. "Happy Valentine's Day."

Me: "Oh thank you! But I don't have anything for you. I forgot all about it. I'm really sorry."

He shrugged. "Doesn't matter. As long as you'll be my valentine." Then he kissed me on the cheek.

My heart leaped. I looked around quickly to see if anyone was watching. The coast was clear so I kissed him. On the lips. He sniffled. I noticed he was coming down with a cold. So I backed off. "Uh-oh. Bad cold. Guess you'll have to settle for one kiss."

He nodded. "Yeah. It's a pain. Nothing serious."

Me: "I'll have to hide these chocolates. Don't know what Daddy would say. He doesn't believe in celebrating Valentine's Day."

He opened a window and lit a cigarette. "Your daddy's real strict about lots of stuff, isn't he?"

I knew what he was getting at. But I wasn't about to go there. "Daddy taught us to obey Yashua's law, and no one else's"

Karl: "How you holding up these days?"

Me: "Okay. Did you see the cool booby traps we set?"

Karl: "Sure did. You must be pretty scared what with all that talk about kidnapping."

I shrugged. "Not very. It doesn't seem real."

Karl: "Seen or heard anything?"

Me: "Not a thing."

Karl: "Anybody keeping watch at night?"

Me: "We sleep at night."

Karl: "You need someone out here watching their movements at night. The feds probably got posts all over out there."

Me: "We've been all through those woods. There's nothing out there."

Karl: "Gotta know what you're looking for. They're good at hiding their tracks. I've been trained. I know what to look for."

Me: "What are you getting at?"

Karl: "I've been thinking real hard about this whole thing since the kidnapping came up. I've decided to offer to stay on here. And help keep watch."

I actually laughed. "You might be decided. But my daddy's a whole nother story. He'll never allow it." He started coughing and hacking over the cigarette smoke, so I said, "We better get on out of here before we get caught."

I tucked the box of chocolates in the waistband of my sweat pants, underneath my shirt and headed for the house.

Before they left, Karl opened his big mouth in front of the grown-ups. I couldn't believe it. He made a little speech about his concern for our family's safety and offered to stay on and keep watch at night.

"That's out of the question!" Shelly said immediately.

Daddy's reaction really surprised me. "Young man, I think we all know whose safety you're most concerned about here." He looked at me. I, of course, turned bright red. "That's a very generous offer. We'll think it over while you get rid of that nasty cold. You might want to take into consideration that we don't allow cigarette smoking around here."

It was Karl's turn to get red in the face. When he glanced at me, I stuck my tongue out at him. I know it was silly. But I couldn't resist.

After they left, Shelly spoke her mind to Daddy against Karl staying here. Luckily she kept my name out of it. Or I would've told him right then and there about her gossiping.

All he said was, "You spoke your mind. But it just might come to that. We might need more help keeping this place secure. We have to think of the children."

Myself, I don't know what to think. Shelly has a point. It's hard enough as it is to find a little speck of privacy around here. I can't imagine what it would be like to have Karl around here all the time. But Daddy's right about security. Karl made a strong argument for someone keeping watch at night. It's all so confusing.

Oh well. Daddy said nothing's going to be decided right away. So I have plenty more nights to sleep on it. And so I shall.

Good night Juniper. Wherever you are.

Your friend,

Sarah

Thursday, February 20

Dear Juniper,

I guess I must've picked up that cold bug Karl had. Tonight my throat really hurts. My head aches and I've had this stuffy nose all day. All I feel like doing is sleeping. Except I have to blow my nose a lot. So I have mountains of hankies to wash out. Ugh.

I was listening to a talk show on the radio today. Rush Limbaugh. Daddy and Shelly usually listen. Sometimes I do, too. Anyway, he was talking about abortion so naturally I was interested. Daddy's pro-life. He says abortion is a sin. The Bible says only Yashua gives life.

Sometimes on the show, people call in to talk about the topic. This woman called today. She told about how she was pro-life. But her daughter was raped a year ago when she was only 12. She actually became pregnant. The caller said she couldn't force her little girl to bear a child. Then she started crying.

Daddy said, "Two wrongs don't make a right. If something like that happened to Sarah, it would be Yashua's will that she have the baby. We'd raise it as if it was our own."

I could hardly believe my ears. What about me? I'm the one who'd have to go through all the pain and misery. Rape is horrible enough without being forced to have a baby. I mean, 12 years old is too young to have a baby. Or get married. It might be too young to go steady. Even that's not all it's cracked up to be.

The caller talked about how she loved her daughter more than life itself. She said forcing her daughter to have the baby would've been like raping her of her childhood, just like she was raped of her innocence.

See the story was, the babysitter's boyfriend raped the daughter and the babysitter both, one night while the caller was at work. It must've been horrible. She said she helped her daughter get an abortion and she's never been sorry for it.

Afterward Daddy was all riled up about the whole thing. "People should learn to trust Yashua's law. There was good reason for that daughter to bring a child into the world. The Bible says sacrifice is the reminder of Sin, but Yashua's law is the shadow of good things to come. If she didn't trust Yashua's law in the first place, she left herself and her daughter open to the devil's work."

Now I don't know anymore. Daddy says pro-life is Yashua's Law. But if something so wicked as rape ever happened to me, I'd expect Daddy would want to spare me from suffering even more.

The caller was a mom. Maybe moms and dads see things differently when it comes to daughters. Even if his daughter gets raped, maybe the dad still sees her as sacred, and likewise any baby that comes from her as sacred. When all the mom sees is how her own baby has been defiled in the worst way, and she just wants to help her get rid of the pain.

I wonder what it must be like, Juniper. To know the love of a mom, who would move heaven and earth to spare her child the pain of wicked sin. A mom who would truly lay down her life. There is something so absolutely divine in that.

However, thinking about all of this only serves to deepen my loneliness. Lately it seems I bump into so many things that don't make as much sense as they used to. And I don't know what it all means. No matter what Daddy said, I always accepted it. Now it seems I'm forced to question everything.

Even after all these years, I still miss my mommy. For some reason, since I started writing these letters to you, I think about her a lot more than I ever used to. I know what daddy says about the sin of the divorce, and how bad it was when my mommy died. Before all that happened, we were happy. Life wasn't as hard back then as it is now. We weren't living like separatists, that's for sure. We had electricity, and indoor plumbing.

I can remember my mommy worked. She wore pretty suits to the office where she sold houses. Once I heard her and Daddy arguing about our house on Bird of Paradise Lane. Mommy didn't want to sell it. I jumped in and took her side against Daddy, because I didn't want to leave my swing set with the huge barrel slide. I used to worry the divorce was my fault.

To tell you the truth, I don't think Daddy liked that Mommy sold houses. I think it was the bigger reason for the divorce. Daddy didn't work much in those days. He stayed home and took care of me and Abraham. And argued with Mommy a lot.

Suddenly I don't feel very good. Probably I'm just tired. Thanks for putting up with all my ramblings on.

Good night Juniper. Wherever you are.

Your friend,

Sarah

Tuesday, March 3

Dear Juniper,

It's Joseph's birthday. He's two now. He's also really sick. He got the cold bug I had. Only he got way more sick. He started out the same as me with a sore throat and stuffy nose. Then yesterday he started screaming and holding his hands over his ears. His cough sounded like when Yeller barks. Today it seemed like he cried all day.

Daddy went out on patrol with the boys so I had to do Shelly's chores while she took care of the baby.

After they left, she chewed my butt about giving Joseph the bug. "This is all your fault. Don't think for one minute I didn't see you and Karl out in that pickup truck."

Me: "I don't know what you're talking about."

It was a lie because I figured she was talking about Valentine's Day. But I wasn't about to admit anything.

Shelly: "Karl came here with a cold bug last Friday. Then you got it. I saw the two of you necking in front seat of his father's truck. You can just bet your Daddy's gonna hear about this."

Well Juniper, I had no choice. I had to hold something over her head.

Me: "If you tell Daddy on me, I'll tell him what Karl told me about the Order thinking he made a deal with the feds to get out of jail."

Shelly: "We've been down this road before. You just keep your mouth shut."

Me: "I think he has the right to know."

Shelly: "Of course he would, if there was any truth to it. But there isn't."

Me: "How do you know that?"

Shelly: "Just look at how the members of the Order treat us. The Fishers. The Slocumbs. They bring our mail and supplies. They buy eggs. What better friends could we ask for? They even hired a lawyer. Your daddy can't afford that. And don't you think that lawyer would've found out by now if your daddy took money from the feds? It just isn't true."

Me: "Maybe that's why the Order hired that Lawyer in the first place. So they could spy on Daddy, too. Just like the Feds. Daddy has the right to know what's going on."

Shelly: "Get it through that thick head of yours, Sarah Smith. There's nothing going on. Believe me. If there was, I'd know about it. Repeating rumors to your Daddy will only serve to get him more riled up than he already is. Just leave it alone."

Me: "Then don't you go telling Daddy that it's my fault Joseph's sick. You just leave my friendship with Karl alone."

Shelly: "Well mark my words, young lady. No way will Karl Fisher be staying on here, like your own personal bodyguard. I won't allow it. But if you expect me to keep your little secret, then you can just go and strip all the beds, wash the sheets and hang them out on the clothesline."

I swear, nothing fazes that woman. So I did as I was told.

Washing those sheets turned into a fiasco. I caught Abraham and Travis out back, tossing eggs at the crows that come and steal the corn around the chicken coop. The way I feel about eggs these days, I just laughed at first. But eggs are like nuggets of gold to Shelly. I knew she'd be furious. So I bribed them to help me hang out the sheets. Those geeks dropped one in the mud underneath the clothesline. Of course it was my top sheet. And I had to wash it all over again. Now as I lay here, my sheets are cold and rough from hanging out in the damp March wind under an overcast sky. The top sheet doesn't feel quite dry. It's very uncomfortable.

Anyway, I'm super tired from all of this upheaval. I don't think Shelly will say anything to Daddy about me and Karl. For now anyway.

Good night Juniper. Wherever you are.

Your friend,

Sarah

Saturday, March 7

Dear Juniper,

So much has happened this week. I haven't even had the chance to write it all down until tonight.

Shelly can't blame me and Karl anymore for giving Joseph the bug. One by one this week everybody around here has gotten sick. First Travis, then Daddy and Abraham. Shelly came down with it on Thursday.

The worst part was that Joseph didn't get better like he was supposed to. In fact he woke up screaming in the middle of the night on Thursday. By the time Karl and Mr. Fisher came by with supplies on Friday, little Joseph was coughing and puking.

Shelly said he needed to see the doctor in Sandpoint. Mr. Fisher offered to drive them. In her rush to leave, she wasn't paying any attention when Karl stayed behind.

Daddy noticed. After they left, he said to Karl, "Thanks for staying, son. Both my boys are too sick to go out on patrol. And Sarah needs to tend to them. That leaves me to make the rounds. Sure could use some company."

Karl: "Sounds like you've got a bad cough there yourself. I can go out alone, if you're not up to it."

Daddy insisted on going. While they were gone I found a can of pineapple rings in the cupboard. So I chopped them up and baked pineapple walnut muffins. No raisins.

Daddy was all smiles upon their return. "You'll never guess what this one found out there on the west trail."

Karl held up a thing that looked like a small video camera.

Me: "What's that?"

They gobbled hot muffins. Between bites, Karl told me, "It's a surveillance camera. Found it in a tree when I climbed up to show your daddy some of the feds' stakeout maneuvers."

Daddy: "Sure enough, he spotted one of their nests. This young man is well trained. He knows his stuff when it comes to covert activity."

Karl gulped his muffin and nearly choked. I poured him a glass of water.

Daddy kept on talking. "You got sharp sites, son. We could use some eagle eyes around this place. That camera was no more than 500 yards from here."

142

After all the excitement, Daddy must've forgotten all about Shelly's rule to never let the boys gather eggs. He sent them out to the chicken coop this morning. I don't know what happened, but we found one of Shelly's prize Rhode Island Reds limping around the yard this afternoon. So Daddy went out and killed it, dressed it, and brought it in for me to put in the oven for supper.

Me: "Shelly's going to be awful mad about this."

Daddy: "Couldn't be helped. The bird got out and got itself injured somehow."

Shelly and Mr. Fisher got back just before dark. Joseph had fallen asleep on the ride back from Sandpoint. And Shelly was feeling quite poorly herself.

"The baby has strep throat," she told us. "At the clinic they did one of those 10 minute throat cultures. Except it took three hours. The Doctor gave him a shot. Then we had another hour wait at the Walmart pharmacy for the antibiotic prescription."

I groaned. "You went to Walmart? I haven't set foot in there since last summer."

Karl looked at me and raised his eyebrows. I guess he never stopped to think about how isolated we've been.

When we all finally sat down for supper, after the prayer Shelly just looked at the roasted chicken. "Where did this come from?"

Daddy: "One of the chickens got out and got injured somehow."

Shelly: "So you killed it? What was wrong with it anyway? Who let it out?"

Daddy: "Doesn't matter anymore. Good meat's been scarce this winter. And growing kids need protein. Besides that, tomorrow you can make up a batch of chicken soup for all the sick ones around here. It's Yashua's will."

She stood up. "If it's meat you want, then send the boys out hunting. You're not going to kill off anymore of my prize Rhode Island Reds!"

She marched off to her bedroom without so much as touching the meal I fixed. She completely missed the conversation between Daddy and Mr. Fisher.

Daddy: "That son of yours knows a thing or two about covert operations. I was duly impressed at the way he zeroed in on that FBI camera today. But that also means they're closing in on us. He offered to stay and keep watch once before. I think the time has come to take him up on his offer."

Mr. Fisher agreed and so it was decided. Karl will become the night watchman around here. Last night he slept a couple hours at a time on the sofa downstairs to build up his stamina for staying awake more hours at a time. I had to slide the fabric trunk in front of the loft railing and stack some books on top in order to have more privacy. Tonight he's out on patrol as I'm writing this.

Of course Shelly was even more livid when she found Karl here this morning.

She cornered me in the kitchen and scolded me. "No one gave you permission to use those pineapple rings for muffins. It just so happens I was saving them for the Easter ham. As penance I'm taking the cost out of your allowance."

Then she mouthed off to Daddy about going over her head about Karl.

All he said was, "Not once have I heard you volunteer to go out on patrol during the night, and pluck surveillance cameras out of trees. Therefore I suggest you keep your opinions to yourself. The decision's already been made."

She retreated to the bedroom again. She and Joseph are both still sick. Now she's really mad, so we didn't see much of either of them all day.

I was the one who ended up making the chicken soup Daddy wanted.

The hardest part is his new rule that Karl has to escort us to the outhouse at night. It's kind of embarrassing. I don't think I'll ever get used to it. Otherwise I kind of like having him around. He's like a comrade. I mean, usually I'm either getting my butt chewed by Shelly, like some stupid little kid, or else I'm supposed to babysit my brothers and act like a grown-up. With Karl I can pretty much just be myself.

As nervous as I am about this new arrangement, it's brought some real excitement into my life for a change. But it's time to blow out the candle. I don't need to have Karl come back inside and start asking a lot of questions about what I'm doing up here so late.

Good night Juniper. Wherever you are.

Your friend,

Sarah

Monday, March 16

Dear Juniper,

Joseph started feeling better from the antibiotic right away. But Shelly kept on babying him, using him as an excuse to make me do all the work. After supper dishes, supper which I had to cook. And dishes I had to do. Except Abraham helped me. Shelly told me to take Joseph and get him ready for bed.

I have to admit, I was feeling super cranky by then. So I sassed her. "What am I? The nanny, too?"

Shelly: "Well it's the least you can do for making your little brother so sick."

Me: "For the last time, I never had strep throat. He didn't get it from me!"

Should've kept my big mouth shut. After I put Joseph to bed, she banished me to the loft for sassing. Right in front of Karl. Like I'm some snot-nosed little kid.

Anyway, it took awhile before Daddy let me go on patrol with Karl and the boys. He lets me go along whenever he goes. I take the boys myself in the mornings while Karl is sleeping in.

148

I figure Shelly must've given Daddy the notion she didn't want me and Karl together out of her sight. As a matter of fact when she got to feeling better last week she accompanied me to the outhouse and chewed my butt whole way.

"I see you've been behaving yourself just fine with Karl Fisher around here. You've been a big help with chores, what with all the sickness. But I reckon that's just to impress your young man. I don't put much stock in it. So I'm warning you ahead of time, when the work slacks off I don't want any funny business between the two of you. I'm not about to raise up any bastard of yours."

Well Juniper, she insulted me to tears. I snapped back, "You have your own little bastard to take care of."

She shot me a wicked glance and smacked me across the face. I ducked inside the outhouse and locked the door. I composed myself and she was gone when I came out. We never said another word about it.

This afternoon I went along to patrol the north trail with Karl and the boys. To tell you the truth, we've spent less time alone together since he came to stay. I guess he must've noticed because he started right in, his usual plucky self. Just as soon as the boys ran off ahead.

First he lit a cigarette, which he's had no trouble keeping up with on midnight patrol, in spite of Daddy's rule.

Karl: "Your mom doesn't much like me staying here."

Me: "She's not my mom."

Karl: "She sure acts like it."

Me: "She used to be a lot more fun. Ever since this whole thing happened with Daddy. The warrant and the arrest and all. She's been acting crazier and crazier."

Karl: "So what's that got to do with you or me?"

Me: "It's probably just me. I think she's having a hard time with me growing up. She can't control me as much as she used to. I stand up to her. And she doesn't like that."

Karl: "But you work your butt off around here."

I thought about what Shelly said about that. At least he noticed. I shrugged.

He put his arm around me. "I never realized what a bitch it is for you being sequestered up here like this."

Me: "It's not so bad since you came to stay."

Karl: "You must be pretty much relieved you don't have to go out to that birthing shed anymore. I've never heard of such a thing. I'd never force my wife out to some old shed. I mean, your monthly isn't that bad. Is it?"

Suddenly I pulled away from him. "I don't want to talk about it."

He came over and put his hands on my shoulders. "I can't stand to think you could've been kidnapped out there."

It was all too embarrassing. I pulled further away. "You heard what I said."

He grabbed me and kissed me. Right then I heard Yeller and the boys crashing through the woods. So we separated. But not before he stole one more kiss.

As usual we reported that we didn't see anything out on the trail. In fact, ever since Karl found the surveillance camera in the treetop, we haven't found so much as a footprint. Daddy says the feds've backed off. I hope he's right.

I could never tell this to anyone but you. I had a dream last night. Usually I never remember my dreams. But this one was so vivid. I was out hiking on one of trails by myself. No weapon.

My foot got tangled in a booby trap. The feds captured me. I was scared to death. But they were all smiles and laughing. Like it was a big joke. All of a sudden Daddy was there. And Karl. They were laughing right along with the feds. Like they were in on the joke. I didn't understand what the joke was all about. But I didn't care because the trouble was all gone. And that was all that mattered to me.

One thing's for sure, I'm not as scared with Karl around. Think I'll make another trip to the outhouse so I can see him once more before bed.

Your friend,

Sarah

Saturday, March 21

Dear Juniper,

Hannah and the Slocumbs came by today. At first I was so glad to see her. It had been such a long time. Then once we had the chance to talk alone together I guess I changed my mind. As far as I'm concerned, talking to her only added to the trouble.

Anyway, she thought the whole idea of going out on patrol sounded like fun. So she went out on the east trail with me and the boys. Karl was still sleeping in. He'd been up all night chasing flashlights out on the south trail.

Hannah was practically bursting with gossip. She could hardly wait to tell me. "Everybody's wondering why your dad didn't show up for his court date last week."

I was stunned. Naturally, I'd forgotten all about it. I never knew the exact date anyway. But I pretended like I knew everything she was talking about. "I think maybe they changed that. He's got a lawyer now, you know."

Hannah: "Of course I know. My dad was the one who hired him. They had a secret meeting of the Order at our house

153

last week. I heard them talking, Sarah. It didn't sound too good. Some of the men are mad because they hired that lawyer. They say your dad's not cooperating."

Me: "That's not true. It's just that the feds told Daddy we could lose this property. Then they lied about the court date in the newspaper."

Hannah: "Well whatever. I don't even know myself what's true. Except some of the men said they thought your Dad wouldn't have the guts to miss his court date unless the feds paid him off."

Me: "My daddy didn't take money from the feds. Go ask Karl. He wondered the same thing. Now he knows better."

Hannah just shrugged. "I never said I believed it. I'm just telling you because it scared me. My mom thinks you and Shelly and the boys should come stay with us for a few days."

Me: "I wish we could. Except it is kind of exciting with Karl around here now."

We talked about him and giggled over his accompanying me to the outhouse.

Of course Hannah already knew about the feds' plan to kidnap me from the birthing shed. Like I said, gossip travels through the Camp like wild fire. I'm still so embarrassed. I can't help it. How will I ever face my friends again?

In my own mind I was half ready to dismiss all Hannah had said to me about the Order and Daddy.

Then right before they left, I overheard Mrs. Slocumb urging Shelly, "Think hard about what I said. You've had quite a time of it up here, already. Just pack up the kids and spend a few days with us. You'll be safe inside the Camp."

But, it didn't sound to me like she'd told Shelly about the secret meeting of the Order. I wondered why. I shuddered.

For the first time I can actually feel the danger tonight. It troubles me that I'm stuck with the burden of this information. It's so close to what Karl was warning me about after Daddy's arrest.

I don't exactly know why Daddy didn't go to court last week. Maybe I should talk to Karl first. Maybe my daddy said something to his dad about it.

I'm so confused. I don't want to be involved in this at all.

I feel caught in the middle of something I don't really understand.

I need to pray for Yashua's guidance.

Pray for me, Juniper. Wherever you are.

Your friend,

Sarah

Wednesday, March 25

Dear Juniper,

Daddy always says, when it rains it pours. It rained all day today.

I've been forced to put off doing anything about the information Hannah told me about the Order. All of a sudden things are really happening around here.

In the past I've mentioned the booby traps we've been setting. We use nylon fish line and string it across the trail, tied around two trees. Then if the line is broken, we check for footprints or other signs of intruders. Up until last weekend, not one of our lines had ever been disturbed. Not even so much as a deer had tripped a one of them. But ever since Sunday, every last one has been snapped.

This morning, Karl stayed awake and ate pancakes with Daddy so they could talk about the situation. I kept myself busy nearby in the kitchen so I could listen in.

Karl: "Lines were all snapped again this morning. Even the new ones. Dang feds must be all over the place."

Daddy: "How the hell do they get past us?"

Karl: "Those dudes are well trained. Very sophisticated. Bet they've got night vision goggles. No other explanation. The only flashlights I've seen were out on the south trail the other night."

Daddy: "We can't have them coming in and surrounding us like sitting ducks."

Karl: "You're right. They could be out there setting booby traps of their own, for all you know. I say move to the next level. Set your traps to do some damage."

Daddy: "What kind of damage are we talking about? I got two young sons traipsing through those woods, remember."

Karl: "Just one or two strategically placed traps. If the boys help us set them, they'll know how to avoid them."

Apparently Karl has not yet spent sufficient time around those two geeks to know how much trouble they can get themselves into without even trying. I didn't say much about it until I went out with them this afternoon. Karl's plan for a damaging new trap turned out to be just a fancy snare tied to a tree branch overhead.

"You aren't exactly going to do much damage with that," I joked.

Karl hadn't had enough sleep so he just sneered at me. We set snares on the north, west and east trails, using the closest tall tree to the clearing where the house stands. The trees aren't many or tall enough on the south trail, which is closest to the driveway.

Anyway on a lighter note, gardening begins once again, even in the mud and slush of March. Mr. Fisher brought out some peat pots last Friday. Tomorrow we will transplant all the tiny new seedlings we sprouted into pots. Daddy already put up the shelves by the wood stove in front of the window. This might seem strange to you, but somehow the thought of planting new vegetables gives me hope. Hope for spring. Hope for tomorrow. I pray we will soon be released from this prison.

Your friend,

Sarah

Thursday, March 26

Dear Juniper,

What a day this has been! I thought for sure Shelly was going to have her way and send Karl packing when his daddy comes tomorrow. I guess you might say I'm partially responsible for his pardon.

It all started right after supper. While planting seedlings today I came to a decision about Hannah's gossip. I planned to talk to Karl. I figured maybe if he was at least standing right there when I told Daddy, he wouldn't get so riled up. Things didn't work out that way, wouldn't you know.

After supper, I told Shelly, "Leave the dishes until I get back. I'm going for a walk."

But she must've read my mind. "Oh no you don't, young lady. Dalton, pay attention. This is a perfect example of what's going on around here behind your back."

Daddy was getting his Bible study materials together. "What're you all riled up about now, woman?"

Shelly: "It's these two. Sarah just told me to leave the supper dishes while she goes out for a walk. Sure enough, you can bet Karl will follow suit and meet her behind one of the outbuildings so they can neck."

Karl sat at the table drinking coffee. He turned all red in the face.

Daddy: "What in the name of Yashua are you talking about?"

Shelly: "Are you so blind you can't see the nose in front of your face?"

Daddy: "I can see my nose just fine, thank you. And from where I'm standing I can also see that Karl has been no less than a gentleman around Sarah."

"Ha!" Shelly flailed her arms wildly. "That's what you think. Just today Travis told me he saw the two of them necking out on the trail last week. In front of the boys, Dalton."

Daddy: "Is this true?"

Me and Karl just looked at each other, kind of like in shock. I don't think he realized Travis spied on us that day. I know I sure didn't.

Shelly: "Of course it's true. This is just exactly the reason why I never wanted him staying here. With my own eyes I saw the two of them necking in the front seat of Fisher's pickup last month. I say it's time we send him back home where he belongs."

Well, I wasn't nearly as ashamed as I was angry. Shelly should've kept her big mouth shut. That was definitely the last straw for me.

Karl stood up right then. No doubt to take his punishment.

But I stepped forward instead. "Forget the walk. Anyway, all I wanted to do was get up the courage to tell you what Hannah said to me last Saturday. I know how much you hate gossip. It's just that this is something you'll probably want to hear."

Karl just looked at me kind of strange.

Daddy: "Well I reckon that's for me to decide. Out with it then."

I took a deep breath and told him the whole story about everyone wondering why he missed the court date. That the Order is mad because they hired the lawyer. That some of them

162

suspect the feds paid him off so he didn't have to go to court. And I concluded with, "Hannah said she even heard one of them say that pretty soon we'll be hearing the charges have been dropped."

Daddy kept silent for a long time.

Shelly muttered to me, "I can't believe you did this, you little troublemaker."

Finally Daddy looked at Karl. "What do you know about this?"

Karl: "I never heard about their latest meeting. I did know some members of the Order were suspicious that you were taking money from the feds for information on their activities."

Daddy: "Who are they, son?"

Karl: "You know I can't give you names, sir. That would be a violation of code. But I can guaran-damn-tee you that it's not me or my dad. We're on your side."

"There are no sides between me and the Order!" Daddy's voice thundered. "The only enemy is the beast government." He paused. "So now I see clearly. The feds must be planting these lies on purpose in order to turn everyone against me."

Karl: "That's the way I see it, sir."

"Exactly!" Daddy looked at Shelly. "Don't you see? If we send Karl home it will seem to the Order like we're trying to hide something. If he stays, they think they've got their very own spy. Karl here, is our only link to them. And he knows full well who the enemy is."

Karl just nodded and stared at Daddy. To tell you the truth Juniper, Karl's not such a big shot Nazi these days. I think him getting in the middle of this whole thing with Daddy is a lot more than he ever bargained for.

But that wasn't even the end of it. Daddy accompanied me to the outhouse afterward and chewed my butt about Karl. "The Bible says the unmarried woman careth for the things of Yashua, that she may be holy both in body and in spirit. Remember Eve in the Garden of Eden, Sarah. Because you are woman, and the very essence of woman is evil, your presence is like a serpent of temptation for young Karl. It is up to you to turn away that serpent. See to it that you do not misbehave around him."

I didn't exactly know what to say. So I kept my mouth shut. I figured I'd said enough for one day. Honestly, I never thought Daddy would approve of Karl kissing me. Or going steady. But it seems so unfair to blame it all on me. I guess I would've thought Daddy would feel more protective of me as his virgin daughter. Or at least thank me for telling him about the Order's suspicions. Instead he proclaimed me as the evil temptress. It was both frustrating and embarrassing. And I don't understand.

Before bedtime, he called us around the table for Bible study.

Even Karl. Daddy stood up and read Ezekiel 7:25-26. "Destruction cometh; and they shall seek peace, and there shall be none. Mischief shall come upon mischief, and rumor shall be upon rumor, then shall they seek a vision of the prophet; but the law shall perish from the priest, and counsel from the ancients."

I have no clue what it means but he told us all to ponder it. I guess that's Daddy's way of saying what he thinks about

Hannah's gossip. It's just another part of the problem. We have to put our faith in Yashua.

Anyway, he sent us up to bed early. I didn't mind because it gave me more time to write to you. Now it's late and I'm tired.

Good night Juniper. Wherever you are.

Your friend,

Sarah

Friday, April 3

Dear Juniper,

We had ourselves quite a scare today. Ever since Daddy let Karl stay on here four weeks ago, Mr. Fisher has been arriving pretty early every Friday with supplies.

I have to admit by lunch time when Karl came down from the loft all sleepy eyed, and asked, "Where's my dad?" we were all wondering the very same thing. Mr. Fisher hadn't shown up yet.

Lunch was split pea soup and peanut butter sandwiches. We were really counting on Mr. Fisher to bring more food.

Karl: "Think I'll take a hike out on the south trail this afternoon. You can see the road for quite a ways up there. In case he had a flat tire. Or something."

Daddy: "You'll be exposed. Anyone can see you from the road."

"I'll go with him," I offered without thinking. "It'll just look like we're taking a walk."

Shelly glared at me first, then Daddy.

So he said, "You boys go on along. Take Yeller. And stay together, no matter what."

I looked at them. "Just make sure you boys mind what Daddy says."

They nodded and grinned their usual mischievous grins.

In case you don't remember, the south trail is the one that follows the driveway. It's a steep, rocky trail down to Meadow Ridge Road. Karl took along his 9mm. Of course the boys had their rifles. But I left my gun at home. Even though Daddy wants us to, I don't carry mine anymore. Doesn't make sense. I don't want to get shot. And I don't plan on shooting anyone. Even if they are feds.

It didn't take us long at all to discover what was keeping Mr. Fisher from getting to our place. As we hiked over the blind spot on the ridge, we could see the broad creek valley below. And the roadblock at the bottom of our driveway.

"Ho-lee shit," Karl muttered.

I grabbed Yeller by the collar just in case he got any big ideas about barking and taking on the feds his own self. Otherwise the four of us just stood and stared dumbfounded at

168

the whole army right there in front of us. The armored tank was the very first thing I saw, parked sideways across the turn off to go up the driveway.

I must admit it took me awhile to get past that. To really see all the men and vehicles parked down there. Besides the tank, there were two black Suburbans, one black Jeep, and at least a dozen men dressed in black uniforms. It was hard to count with them moving around so much.

The sun was shining. The air was warm. Probably 60 degrees. But for some reason I just started shivering. A couple of the men below started looking through binoculars. That seemed to jar Karl out of his own daze.

He glanced around and whispered, "We better get down before they spot us."

I nodded and crouched next to Yeller. He was whimpering a little, but mostly because he didn't like me holding his collar. Karl frog walked over to the boys who were still spellbound by the awful sight.

He tugged them down to their knees and hissed, "Shh!"

We just sat there watching for what seemed like a long time. My arm went numb from holding onto Yeller. But it didn't seem to matter. None of us moved a muscle.

What were we waiting for? I kept thinking we'd see one of the men do something to give away their intentions. Perhaps Karl was waiting to see if his daddy was going to drive up the road. Travis and Abraham were no doubt fascinated by the huge tank, scary as it was.

I was the one who eventually whispered, "We better go tell Daddy."

Karl nodded. We followed him silently back up the trail, knees bent, heads bowed. As far as we knew, we weren't spotted. The boys ran yelling all the way back to the house. I finally let go of Yeller and he tore off after them, barking.

I stayed behind with Karl. "What do you make of this?"

Karl: "Nothing good. That's for sure. Guess they mean to cut off all your contact with the outside world."

Me: "Yours too. You're just as trapped here as we are."

He didn't say anything. We saw Daddy and Shelly on the porch then, surrounded by two riled up boys. Karl jogged ahead

170

to meet him. By the time I caught up, he'd pretty much filled them in on the bad news.

Karl: "I'll head out on the west trail tonight. If I make it all the way to the road, then we'll know there's at least one way out."

Shelly: "Don't even bother. You can bet they've got us surrounded."

Daddy nodded. "Anyhow we're not looking for a way out."

Karl: "If you don't mind my saying so, sir, if the west trail is open to the road, I suggest we make a plan to hike on out of here. The Order'll hide you folks down at the Camp."

Daddy just looked at him. "That's a mighty big promise. On whose authority do you make such an offer?"

Karl bowed his head and shuffled his feet. "I would expect they'd help you, sir."

Daddy: "You heard Sarah's gossip about the Order. They don't trust me. Why would they help me now?"

Karl: "Because we ask them to, sir. They're your only hope."

"Yashua is our only hope, son," Daddy proclaimed. "Put your faith in Yashua, and eternal life is yours. Put your faith in men, and you will surely die. As for me and my family we will stay and fight. Our future is in Yashua's hands."

Karl shrugged and walked away. I couldn't go after him right then to find out what he was thinking because Daddy made me and the boys go around and padlock all the outbuildings. We've been keeping things locked up during the night since Karl came to stay. Looks like the same goes for daytime now. Karl seemed very solemn and kept to himself the rest of the day.

After supper tonight Daddy said, "It's just a matter of time before the feds roll that tank up our driveway and mow us down in our own home." He took up his Bible and read, "Yashua will not suffer you to be tempted above that ye are able, but will make a way to escape, that ye may be able to bear it."

Me: "Maybe that means Yashua wants us to hike out of here if the west trail is open."

Daddy: "It most certainly does not! Listen to the word. Yashua will make a way to escape. Not Karl Fisher. Not the men of the Order. But Yashua. We will await his guidance."

Later when Karl walked me to the outhouse before bed, we finally had a chance to talk.

While he smoked a cigarette I confided, "If it makes any difference, I happen to like your plan. I'm sure the Slocumbs would take us in."

Karl shook his head. "I don't know. Maybe your daddy's right. He knows this country's too rough to hike in one night. It's ten miles to Bonners Ferry at least."

Me: "I know where there's an abandoned barn. On the Old Sawmill Road. A couple miles off Meadow Ridge. Me and the boys used to hike down there and shoot grouse. Before all this stuff happened. It's about an hour's walk. We could all hide out there while you head down to Bonners Ferry. Then you could call your dad for help."

Karl stamped out his cigarette. "You know as well as I do your Daddy won't have any part of it. You heard what he said. He means to stay and fight."

I shivered. "I heard him. But that roadblock down there scares me. I just want to get out of here."

He shrugged. "All I can do is head out there and see if the coast is clear."

Me: "Promise you'll take me with you. Please!"

Karl: "I can't promise you that. Your Daddy'll skin me alive. It's a long shot anyway. I need more time to think."

As I write this tonight, I pray Yashua will indeed help us escape. I pray if Karl is out there on the trail, he finds the way clear for us to hike out of here to safety. Even if the Order didn't trust my daddy before, the roadblock will surely prove they were wrong about him. They will help us. I have to believe that.

Pray for us Juniper. Wherever you are.

Your friend,

Sarah

Saturday, April 4

Dear Juniper,

Another day full of fear and anxiety. Karl has disappeared.

He'd been in the habit of reporting the night's activities to Daddy at the breakfast table, then up to the loft for sleep. However this morning he was nowhere to be found. We even postponed breakfast while we searched everywhere on the property.

Finally while we ate our pancakes, I told Daddy what I was thinking. "I'm afraid Karl headed out on the west trail last night. Maybe the feds caught him. I guess this means we really are surrounded."

That seemed to be Shelly's cue to bang the pans on the stove. "Told you so!"

Daddy: "Did he tell you what his plan was?"

Me: "Only that he still intended to see if the coast was clear to hike out of here."

Shelly slammed the coffee pot down on the counter. "I'll tell you what I think. Karl Fisher is a coward. He ran off. Scared to face the enemy."

Me: "That's not true!"

Daddy: "Even so, that's his perfect right. He's got no beef with the government. This is our own private family matter. He helped us all he could. Now he's moved on."

Me: "No. I don't believe that. He'll come back with a whole army of help. You wait and see."

We didn't have to wait long to find out a whole lot more. A little while later, just as Daddy predicted, the armored tank thundered up our driveway and into the yard. Everyone else grabbed their guns and ran to the windows. A helicopter blasted over the house and hovered above the tank, then flew off.

"Cool!" Abraham and Travis shouted in unison.

I was curled up on the couch, clutching Ginny the cat and we shivered together. I thought surely the feds would ram that tank right through our front door.

Suddenly we heard a man's voice over the loudspeaker. "Dalton Smith! You're under arrest. Surrender your weapons immediately. Come out with your hands in the air."

Daddy yelled out the doorway, "You're gonna have to come on in after us."

There was a long pause. Then, "Your friends, Sam Fisher and his son. We have them in custody. They set you up. Tom Slocumb. Mark Champion. Your friends in the Order. They turned on you. You're completely on your own in this. Don't do this to your family. Save yourselves."

Shelly started crying. The boys scrambled out to the back porch, looking for the helicopter.

The voice echoed across the yard. "The Order used you. They never trusted you. They always believed you were an informant."

Daddy hollered back. "If that's true, then it was you servants of the beast who planted that lie in their heads."

The voice answered, "Why do you think the Fisher boy was staying here? They planted him as their spy. It was their own camera he found in the tree. How do you think he knew where to look? He never believed in your cause."

"That's a damn lie!" Daddy shouted.

The voice continued, "Those men in the Order don't care what happens to you, Dalton. They told us all about the ammunition you got stored up here. They've washed their hands of you. Give yourself up. We'll take your statement. Don't let them do this to you. This is your chance to give us the information we want."

"Damn," Daddy muttered, raking his hands through his hair. "See how they twist and turn the truth around."

Me: "But Daddy! What if it's all true?"

"Shut up, Sarah!" Shelly blubbered. "This is a setup, Dalton. Just like before. They're lying. Don't forget how those people helped us."

"Quiet down, woman!" Daddy shouted.

The voice was silent after that. For the whole rest of the day. Except the tank remained steadfast. And the loudspeaker was anything but silent! Between the feds blaring trashy heavy metal music through it, and the helicopter clattering up and down the ridge, I could barely hear myself think.

We had to pee off the back porch because we were afraid to venture out any further. Every so often the black Jeep ferried men to and from the tank, then disappeared back down the driveway.

I don't know. I suppose this is the end for us, Juniper. I've spent most of the day up in the loft. The noise is no better and no worse up here. I don't know what to think about Karl and the rest of those men in the Order. Maybe the feds were lying.

But what if they were telling the truth? After all, it's not the first time we've heard that the men in the Order don't trust Daddy.

And what about Karl? When I think about him finding the camera, it's easy to see how it could be true. He talked about the feds spying on us. Always asked if I'd seen any around here. The only people I ever saw were Fishers and Slocumbs. Either of those men had plenty of opportunities to bring in and hide a camera. Even Karl himself. They always seemed to know everything that was going on around here all the time.

Except I can't bear to think Karl could betray me. Or maybe all the stuff about going steady and getting married was just so much garbage. A way to get close enough to me so I'd tell him things. Maybe he used me, too. I'll never trust anyone ever again.

I'd better stop now. All's quiet outside. But Daddy's awake and roaming around downstairs, in a restless mood. He's very much on guard lately. Nothing escapes his attention. If he happens to make his rounds and finds me with this candle burning, I'll definitely have some explaining to do.

Pray for us Juniper. Wherever you are.

Your friend,

Sarah

Monday, April 6

Dear Juniper,

After a whole weekend of the feds torturing us with their horrible music and their noisy helicopter, they up and left today. Without another word. The tank just rolled off down the driveway this morning. The helicopter's still around. Sometimes it explodes over our heads. Other times we hear it chopping in the distance.

Daddy spends most of his time poring over the Bible. Or cleaning his guns and stockpiling ammunition around the living room. Like this is the Alamo or something. He stacked the boxes next to each crank-out window. Karl had helped him remove the screens before he left. During the weekend he showed us drills for shooting a gun out the window. When the feds come, he wants us to shoot back. We have to rotate window stations.

I didn't say anything. But I don't plan to shoot back. All the pointing of guns, the anger, the setups, the gossip and mistrust. It all has to stop somewhere. Even if I'm only one person, it's going to stop right here with me.

What I did say to him was, "Daddy, what happens if you turn yourself in?"

Daddy: "Then I'd lose this place for sure. My home. What else has a man got besides his home?"

Me: "You still have your family."

Daddy: "If I surrender now, they'll take every last one of you away from me. I'll go to jail, Sarah. I couldn't live with that. I've done nothing more than obey Yashua's law. I'd rather die a free man."

Me: "Then let me go, Daddy. Just like Karl."

I couldn't believe I said it. Thankfully we were out on the back porch, so no one else heard.

Daddy looked me in the eye. "You a traitor then too, Sarah? Been selling your own secrets to enemy?"

In tears, I gasped. "How can you say such a thing! If Karl is a traitor, then he fooled me just as much as he fooled you."

Daddy put his arm around me. "He didn't fool me, Sarah. But I am sorry he fooled you. Yashua's will is harsh sometimes."

"But I don't want to die," I said sobbing.

Daddy: "Then so shall you live. And we shall all pray for Yashua's guidance."

However, as each day passes our situation grows steadily worse. I'm afraid we'll end up starving to death. We have little food left. Shelly sends the boys out back to sneak in the chicken coop for eggs.

Oh rats. I hear Shelly calling me to come and help with supper.

One by one she's been forced to surrender more prize Rhode Island Reds to put food on the table. For some reason, it bothers her to cook the chicken, so she makes me do it.

Hopefully I can manage to keep writing to you without getting caught. Keep up the prayers. Wherever you are.

Your friend,

Sarah

Thursday, April 9

Dear Juniper,

Today is the saddest day of my life. Unthinkable tragedy has befallen us.

This morning after chores, Daddy sent me and the boys out on patrol to the east trail. "Stay high on the ridge. See if they're coming in from another direction. Whatever you do, stay out of sight. Take your weapons. Be on guard. Prepare to defend yourselves."

We took Yeller with us, as usual. Up until today, we hadn't come across any trouble, so I wasn't exactly nervous about this patrol stuff anymore. Everything was going along fine. Then Yeller and the boys ran off ahead of me, as usual. I figured they were looking to scare up a grouse for dinner. Except what they scared up was more trouble than we could handle.

Travis came running back to me all breathless and pointing down the trail. I quickened my pace and followed him. Soon as we rounded the bend, I saw Abraham standing still in the middle of the trail. He was shouting at someone up ahead. I saw two agents about a hundred yards away. One was partially hidden behind a tree. The other stood in the open. He was dressed in a black uniform and armed with a semiautomatic rifle. I've never wished so desperately for Karl in my life. He would've known exactly what to do.

The agent on the trail shouted, "Drop your gun, boy. Come with me now. No one's going to hurt you."

I heard Abraham holler, "No sir! You won't kidnap me. Like I said! Get off this property or I'll shoot."

"Abraham! No, no, no!" I yelled. "Don't shoot!"

Yeller was growling and pacing at his feet. Then everything happened way too fast. Abraham fired his gun in the air.

"I said drop your gun!" The agent started walking toward him.

But that was all Yeller needed to charge forward, barking madly.

The agent halted. "Get back! Call off your dog!"

Abraham did nothing.

"Yeller! Halt!" I called out.

It was no use. Yeller bit into his pant leg. He raised his gun and fired. Yeller's body flew up in the air and fell back down hard on the ground, and dead. I yanked Travis by the collar and crouched with him behind the tree.

"You shot my dog!" Abraham wailed. Then he did a fool thing. He aimed his gun at the agent.

"Abraham! No! Stop!" I screamed. "Don't shoot!"

He never listens to me. Abraham shot the agent in the leg. He reeled and fell. Then he bolted upright on his good leg and aimed his rifle at Abraham. But as my brother turned to run, a shot rang out. He was thrown back several feet on the trail. Then all was quiet. He didn't move.

In that moment it was as though everything stopped. All the oxygen seemed to have been sucked out of air. I could hardly breathe. There was only the smell. Pungent and acid, like citrus. Only heavier. I didn't know what it was then. But if I ever smell it again, I'll recognize it as death.

Frozen stiff with fear I huddled there with Travis, not knowing whether or not they intended to kill us. Travis' rifle lay flat on the ground under my knee.

186

I could hear them calling back and forth to each other. But my ears were still ringing from the gunfire. I couldn't tell what they were saying. The agent behind the tree came out and helped the wounded guy off the trail into the woods.

Then he hollered, "Go on, you kids! Go tell your mom and dad what happened here. You saw for yourself. The boy shot a man. Tell your Dad what he done by putting a gun in his boy's hands. Tell him to turn himself in before he gets you all killed."

Oh man. That was all the talking to I needed. I grabbed Travis and dragged him back home as fast as I could possibly run.

There I stumbled through the door screaming, "They shot him! They shot him!"

Daddy was reading the Bible at the table. He stood up in alarm while Shelly rushed over and grabbed Travis.

I heard him say, "Abraham ran ahead of us and those two soldiers shot him and Yeller."

"No, no, no. That's not how it happened!" But I was breathing so hard I think I almost fainted.

All I remember is Daddy storming out of the house with Travis. They both took their guns. I felt certain they would be killed. I guess I was crying and fell asleep on the sofa.

The next thing I remember is waking up to Shelly screaming, "Abraham! Abraham!"

I jumped up and ran outside. Daddy was carrying Abraham into the birthing shed. I ran over to him. "What should we do? Should we get a doctor?"

Daddy laid Abraham's frail body on the cot. "Nothing Sarah. He's gone."

Daddy's face was all red and his eyes were swollen from crying. He didn't make a sound. He doesn't cry noisy like me and Shelly. The tears rolled down his face and splashed all over Abraham's bloody shirt, but he never said a word.

Abraham looked so sweet lying there. Daddy told me and Travis to get a pail of water and some towels. We watched him gently remove Abraham's bloody clothes. He washed away all the blood. I couldn't stand to look at the gaping wound anymore so I covered him with a blanket. That very moment when I placed the blanket over his body, I knew the spark of mischief in his eye, and his silly grin were gone forever. He'll always be nine years old. He'll never grow up. He'll never be 12, like me.

Oh Juniper, the page is wet from my tears. I lost my baby brother today. He's in Yashua's hands now. It is little consolation that he crossed over with his best pal, Yeller. We've lost them both. The loss of either one is such a terrible tragedy. Together it seems unbearable.

I should've done something to stop it. If only I had been braver. I shouldn't have hid behind that tree, like a coward. I should've marched over to Abraham, taken his rifle away and surrendered to the feds. At least he would still be alive.

Tonight I told Daddy the truth about what happened out there today on the trail. I begged him to surrender.

Daddy: "I will not surrender, Sarah. But if you must go the way of Karl, that is your choice. As for me, I am prepared to die. Abraham and Yeller were the first. Tomorrow they'll come for the rest of us. We shall arm ourselves and fight our way to death's door."

I guess that was Daddy's way of saying I'm free to leave. Except it means I'd have to walk down to the roadblock and turn myself in. Or let the feds capture me on the trail. What if it's too late to surrender? I'm afraid I'll get shot like Abraham.

Like it or not, I'm trapped here. So if I should happen to die tomorrow, then this is goodbye. Forgive me for never getting these letters mailed to you. I'm sorry I won't ever get to read your letters back to me. To share your hopes and dreams, and all the things that make you happy. I will always regret we never got the chance to meet again, to share the missing pieces of our lives.

Good night Juniper. Wherever you are.

Your friend,

Sarah

Friday, April 10

Dear Juniper,

As you can see I'm still alive. Today is Good Friday, before Easter. There will be no Easter ham for our family this year. For us, or what's left of us, this is Black Friday. It was like a war. Like nothing you could ever imagine. Nor would you ever want to, of that I'm certain.

The feds came back just like Daddy said they would. Everyone was ready with their guns. Except me. As they drove up in their tank and big, black Suburbans, Shelly ordered me to stand guard by the door. But I was too scared. So I refused. All I wanted to do was grab hold of Ginny and go hide under the table.

"Let me take Joseph up to the loft. Please. We can't let anything happen to this baby!" I cried.

Shelly grabbed Joseph with one arm and her rifle in the other and took over the post by the door. "Go on! Go hide out in the coop with the rest of the chickens. That's where you belong!"

191

The feds used the loudspeaker again when they called for Daddy to surrender.

"I'll show them surrender," Shelly grumbled. I'll never know what got into her, but just then she opened the door and fired a warning shot. And she hollered, "Leave this property now! Murderers!"

I was in the midst of retreating up to the loft when I heard another shot and the shattering of glass. I looked over and there lay Shelly. Of course Joseph was screaming. I practically fell down the ladder, then I crawled along the floor over to her. Oh geez, Juniper. Shelly's face was just—gone! When I looked away in horror, I saw blood splashed everywhere. All over Joseph, all over me.

Daddy crawled over to us while I pried the screaming baby from Shelly's arms. It was like they were frozen around his little tummy. I was terrified. Daddy started yelling. He stood up and ran out the door waving his gun. I heard another shot and saw Daddy fall to his knees, sobbing. At first I figured they killed him too. But from where I sat on the kitchen floor, curled up in a ball hanging onto Joseph, I could see through the doorway he'd been shot in the arm. Travis was under the table rocking back and forth, crying. He was soaking wet from where he'd peed his pants.

A whole bunch of feds swarmed through the door right then. Travis reached for his gun but I ordered him to stop. One of the the agents who looked kind of familiar took Joseph away from me.

Another agent helped me to my feet. "Come with me."

"Am-m I ar-r-rested?" My voice trembled from fear.

Agent: "No. But we'll have to find you and your brothers some place to stay."

Me: "Oh. Wait then. Please. Can I get some things? My cat. Please."

He paused like he didn't know if he should trust me.

Me: "I surrender. Honest. That's my gun over there. It's not even loaded. Check for yourself."

He walked over and picked up my gun. "All right then. Make it snappy."

I dashed up to the loft and grabbed the notebook with your letters and Ginny the cat. The agent led me by the arm over to the black Jeep. They took each of us away in separate vehicles. Daddy went in an ambulance. They wouldn't let me talk to him. The same agent who found me with Joseph stayed with me on the long drive to Spokane.

I guess you're the only one I can say this to because you understand me and everything I've been through. Those agents were very nice to me. I was surprised. After all that's happened I should hate them. Except Daddy never taught me to hate. I'd sunk so deep in the clutches of grief and despair. Quite honestly, they seemed to have some kind of unspoken understanding about my feelings. Anyway, they were quiet with me.

The agent told me his name. Agent Duncan. He said he had a daughter about my age. Well, I can tell you I was pretty shocked.

"Is my Daddy going to be all right?" I asked, clutching Ginny. She was pretty scared by then.

Agent Duncan: "Pretty sure. He took a bullet in the arm. Lost some blood. But he should pull through."

Me: "Where are you taking me?"

194

Agent Duncan: "FBI Headquarters in Spokane. From there we'll contact any family or friends for you. Need to find some place you can stay. Got any ideas?"

Me: "I'm sure I can stay with Hannah and the Slocumbs down at the Camp. Do you know who they are?"

"As a matter of fact, we do." He looked over at the other agent riding with him in the front seat and nodded.

I don't know why I thought of the Slocumbs. I guess because of Hannah. After all, it was Mrs. Slocumb who offered to let us come stay before all this happened. In my heart I knew there was no place else to go.

At the FBI place in Spokane, there were TV cameras and reporters everywhere. We had to sneak in the back way. I felt like a celebrity. Before Hannah and Mrs. Slocumb came to get me I gave my notebook full of letters to Agent Duncan.

Me: "I have some letters here in this notebook. They're for a friend of mine. In Florida. Can you take me to the post office by any chance? I'd very much like to send them."

He picked up the notebook and leafed through it. "Letters, huh."

Me: "Please don't read them. It's just that I haven't been to the post office for a long time."

Agent Duncan: "Tell you what. I'll mail these for you. I see you've got the address right here."

Me: "Yes. I can't remember the street number. But I guess if anyone could find that out, it'd be somebody like you. Since you work for the government and all."

Agent Duncan smiled. Before he took the notebook away he paused and looked at me and Ginny. "I'm awful sorry about your brother and your mom. Not to mention the dog. None of this was supposed to happen, you know. We pleaded with your dad to surrender. We gave him every opportunity to answer the charges against him."

My eyes filled with tears but I wiped them away. I wanted to be strong for Daddy. "Shelly's not my mom. I feel bad she's dead. But she's not my mom."

He patted my shoulder. "You gonna be okay?"

I nodded, fighting so hard not to cry.

So here I am tonight at Hannah's house. Mrs. Slocumb was kind enough to come and get us. Joseph and Travis are here, too. They're camped out downstairs in the living room. I'm here in Hannah's room. She and Ginny are asleep next to me. But I can't sleep. Hannah had an extra spiral notebook. She let me have it so I can keep on writing to you. I have more reason now than ever to keep sending you letters. Soon you will get my other letters. I'm sure you'll be anxious to know what's become of me.

By the way, Mrs. Slocumb said Daddy's in the hospital in Spokane. He's going to be okay. But he's being guarded by police officers. He can't have any visitors right now. I don't know when I will finally get to see him. I'm certain he is as full of grief as I am.

It's late. I shouldn't disturb Hannah any longer with this light on. It's been such a strange and terrible day. It's hard to imagine this would be the very same day I'd get to send your letters. I used to think about how happy that would make me. Now I don't know if I'll ever feel happiness again. I've lost everything.

Pray for me Juniper. Wherever you are.

Your friend,

Sarah

Tuesday, April 14

Dear Juniper,

The funerals for Abraham and Shelly both were held today in the Church of Jesus Christ Christian at the Camp. Me and Shelly's boys went along with Hannah and the Slocumbs. Although I've not said much to Mr. Slocumb. I don't know if I should trust him. He hasn't said one word to me about my daddy.

Daddy couldn't come to the funerals. Mrs. Slocumb told me he was moved to the jail in Spokane. I guess that means his arm must be better. I asked if I could see him but she said I'm still not allowed. That made me feel kind of sad.

Everyone in the Camp and then some came for the funerals. They had to turn the TV reporters away at the gate. The service was very nice. I didn't listen real hard because when the minister started talking about Shelly, I got to thinking about how we didn't get along. I suppose if I had stood by the door on Good Friday like she told me, then she wouldn't have been there to shoot at those agents like she did. Maybe she wouldn't't've been killed.

198

If only I had known this was going to happen. If only I had been able to stop it. Maybe if I had turned myself in, then things might've changed just enough so Abraham and Shelly would still be alive.

When they got to Abraham's part of the service, well I just cried and cried like a little baby. It really hit me then how alone I am, with my little brother gone. He was so very young. I'm going to miss him more than anything. I already do. After Mommy died, he was my only real family, except for Daddy. I thought about how I don't even remember my mommy's funeral. I suppose there was one. But I don't think I was there. I don't think I could ever forget something like that.

The hardest thing for me today was all the folks around here telling me what a hero my daddy is. I'm so confused. Don't they know what the Order did to him? Even the Slocumbs. I mean it's nice and all they let me and Shelly's boys stay here like this. Not to mention Ginny the cat. The thing is, I'm like the only one who seems to know the truth. Or else nobody around here wants to admit to the truth. I can't tell.

By the way, Karl was there at the funeral today with the whole Fisher family. He came over to me afterward and said, "Can we go somewhere and talk?"

Me: "Why?"

Karl: "So I can explain what happened that night. I don't want you thinking I deserted you."

I shrugged. "What difference does it make? It's over now. Nothing you say can change what happened."

He grabbed my arm. "I'm sorry, Sarah."

I shook myself free of him and ran all the way to Slocumb's house. Then I just stayed in Hannah's room alone. Anyway, when Hannah came home she found me crying. She'd seen me running away from Karl so of course she thought I was crying over him.

She finally told me the truth about what happened. "Karl told everybody that the feds captured him when he was out on patrol. But I heard my dad and Mr. Fisher talking. There was an inquisition by the Order. That's when Karl confessed that he actually turned himself in. They haven't decided his punishment yet."

200

But it doesn't matter to me anymore, Juniper. So he saved himself. How can I blame him? I was even thinking of doing the very same thing.

I'm very tired tonight. The world weighs heavily on my shoulders. The future is quite uncertain. It's hard not to worry. I can only hope you have received my first notebook of letters by now. For all I know you might be searching for me.

Good night, dear Juniper. Wherever you are.

Your friend,

Sarah

Thursday, April 16

Dear Juniper,

Perhaps one of my prayers will soon be answered.

Before I came up to Hannah's room for the night, Mrs. Slocumb said, "Sarah, I'll be taking you back to FBI Headquarters in Spokane tomorrow."

Me: "Are they going to let me see my daddy?"

Mrs. Slocumb: "I don't know. An Agent Duncan called and said I was to have you in his office tomorrow morning. He didn't give me the chance to ask any questions."

Me: "Well I'm sure it's about my daddy. He probably asked for me."

I can't wait to see him. Maybe he's getting out of jail. I'll bet that's what this is all about. The feds probably told him they were sorry about Abraham and Shelly and Yeller. Then they decided to let him go free. I sure hope his arm is feeling better. I have so many questions to ask him. Like, when can we go back home? Anyway I've made a decision. I don't want to stay with Hannah and the Slocumbs very much longer.

202

Today I told Mr. Slocumb right out, "My daddy never took any money from the feds. He wasn't an informant. I just want you to know that."

Mr. Slocumb: "Well thank you for that, Sarah. But I'm sure your daddy didn't make a habit of telling you every little detail about his business."

Me: "He's in jail right now. How much more proof do you need?"

Mr. Slocumb: "It certainly seems that way. But a lot has happened. What do you say we just leave it at that?"

I don't even think he believed a word I said. So much for my daddy being a hero. They are all a bunch of two-faced bastards.

Which is why I want to go back home as soon as possible. I'm better off up there. I can never feel safe among these people at the Camp who call me and my family "friends." They've been nice enough to me and Shelly's boys. It's true. But those agents were nice too. And if I can't trust the government who's to say I can trust anyone else.

I owe it to Daddy and the memory of Shelly to look after Travis and Joseph. Even though I'm only 12 years old, I can still care for them properly. Although I don't suppose I'll have much say about it in the end. That's why it's so important for me to see him and talk about these things. He'll know what to do.

It's strange, but you feel closer to me at this moment than ever before. I like to think you've received my letters and read them all by now. I'll take some more to Agent Duncan when I go there tomorrow. You can write back to me as this address:

c/o Hannah Slocumb

PO Box 60616

Hayden Lake, Idaho 83835

Hannah will always know how to reach me. Besides you, she's the only friend I have left.

Good night Juniper. I hope to hear from you very soon.

Your friend,

Sarah

Friday, April 17

Dear Juniper,

Even though I didn't get to see my my daddy today, something even more incredible has happened. For both of us! At last we have met. Although it was not what I ever expected in a million years.

My head is still spinning. I only know I need to write this all down. For this whole day has been like a dream, from which I'm still not certain I won't awaken momentarily to return to the nightmare that had become my life.

Mrs. Slocumb drove me to Spokane this morning. At the FBI building, we went straight to Agent Duncan's office.

He said to her, "Sarah's going to be here awhile. Just go on home. We'll be in touch."

Mrs. Slocumb looked at me all concerned. "Will you be all right?"

I nodded.

After she left, I noticed my notebook of letters to you still sitting on his desk. I was so disappointed. "Oh no! You didn't mail my letters."

Agent Duncan: "Actually I did you one better. I made some phone calls instead."

Me: "You called Juniper?"

Agent Duncan: "Not exactly. There's someone I'd like you to see. Just down the hall."

Me: "Is it my daddy?"

Agent Duncan: "No. I'm afraid not. Just follow me."

He took me to a room with a table and some comfortable chairs and a sofa. Like a waiting room. There I met an older man. Kind of like a grandpa, because he had silver hair and shiny, gold glasses. Agent Duncan said his name was Mr. Hale.

"It's so nice to finally meet you," Mr. Hale said to me, like I was famous or something.

Agent Duncan actually left then, which surprised me and got me a little nervous.

Mr. Hale offered me a can of 7Up. "Don't be frightened. I've come a long way to see you."

206

Me: "Who are you?"

Mr. Hale: "That's a very good question. I represent the National Center for Missing and Exploited Children. But the real question here is, who is Juniper Holland?"

Me: "Is Juniper missing?"

Mr. Hale: "I'm not sure. What can you tell me about her?"

I drank some 7Up. "Well, she was my neighbor. My best friend, actually. A long time ago. When I was really little and we lived with my mommy. In Florida. Before she died."

"Your mother died?" he asked. Then he looked up like he was looking at someone behind me. But there was no one there. Just a mirror on the wall. "Is that what your father told you?"

I nodded. "Yes. I was six. Abraham was only three. We were staying with Daddy because it was his turn after the divorce, you see. And that's when our Mommy was killed in the car accident."

He listened real carefully, then he placed a picture on the table. "Look at this photo, please. Can you tell me who this is?"

It was a color picture of a girl about five years old.

Me: "That's Juniper, all right. Where did you get this?"

"Look at this." He handed me another picture of four people. A family type picture. "Do you recognize anyone in this photo?"

I looked more closely. "That's my daddy and my mommy. And that's Juniper. And I think that little boy's name is Austin. But I don't know what they're doing in this picture together."

"Keep looking at the photo," he said very calmly. "Tell me, who is Juniper?"

I pointed to Juniper and then I got this really funny feeling in the pit of my stomach. Of all things I started to cry. Right in front of Mr. Hale, whom I hardly knew. I didn't even know why. So I just blurted out, "I don't feel very good."

"I'm sorry." He patted my hand like a grandpa would. "You're starting to remember. I know it's confusing. And sometimes painful."

208

"Remember? What do I remember?" I really needed him to tell me what those pictures meant. I couldn't for the life of me figure it out.

He pointed to the picture again. "This boy you call Austin, this is your little brother Abraham, at age three. This girl you call Juniper, this is you, at age six. Your name is Juniper Holland."

Well, I thought I was going to jump right out of my skin. He scared me half to death. "How can that be?" I cried.

"Your father took you away. Then he changed your names. For some reason you remembered your old name all these years. Except in your mind, you thought of her as an old friend of yours. It's not an unusual thing to do in your circumstances."

"But Abraham? That doesn't even look like him! Look at the little short pants and the bow tie. He wouldn't be caught dea . . ." But I stopped myself from saying anymore and started sobbing.

Mr. Hale looked past me again and made a motion.

"I'm sorry." He squeezed my hand. "I'm deeply sorry we lost your little brother. And perhaps what I have to tell you now will help with this hurt, just a little. Please, listen very carefully to me." He handed me a Kleenex, which was obviously my cue to stop crying. "Is it all right if I call you Juniper?" he asked.

I blew my nose and shrugged.

Mr. Hale: "You see, Juniper is the only name I've ever known you by. And Austin was your little brother. We've been searching for you for over six years."

Me: "You have? Why?"

Mr. Hale: "Juniper, you were six years old that weekend after Thanksgiving when you and Austin went to stay with your father. Your mother never had a car accident that day. Your mother is alive. She's been trying to find you all this time."

Oh, it was like a miracle! I couldn't speak. Mommy. Alive. Then I thought about Daddy. "What do you mean? Does my daddy know she's alive?"

He nodded. "I'm sorry to be the one to tell you this, but he kidnapped you and Austin. The three of you simply disappeared one day. Your mother's been looking for you ever since. She came to the center and asked for my help. When you gave Agent Duncan your letters to Juniper Holland, he did some investigating. Eventually he called me. Of course I knew who you were. And he told us where to find you."

I took a deep breath. "Well I've heard enough stories lately to last me a lifetime. How can I be sure what's the truth?"

Mr. Hale: "There's someone I'd like you to meet. She's in the next room."

The door burst open and this woman rushed in. She was wearing a pretty lavender suit. I hesitated for an instant to be sure it was truly her. I remembered my mommy had the biggest smile in the whole world. Her mouth and eyes opened wide and turned up at the corners and she glowed with happiness. Even though this woman had tears in her eyes, she smiled exactly the same way. It made me feel all warm inside. There was no doubt about it. She was indeed my mommy. I fled into her arms. She hugged me so tightly I sucked in my breath. My nostrils were filled with the familiar scent of her soft floral perfume. I hadn't smelled perfume in years. Oh how I've missed her so. I never knew how much until today. She was so happy. She wasn't even angry after all these years. She was everything I ever dreamed she was when I was a little girl, and then some.

Daddy always said Yashua giveth and Yashua taketh away. In that moment I felt so blessed, it was as if Abraham was right there. Or Austin. Whoever he was. My little brother seemed to be rejoicing along with me.

Mr. Hale: "As you've probably guessed by now, this is Virginia Holland. Your mother."

"Wait a minute." I thought about her name. Virginia. "Did my daddy used to call you Ginny? Is that your name?"

She smiled. "Why yes! Oh sweetie. You remembered."

Me: "That's my cat's name. Ginny. But Daddy never liked me calling her that. Anyway Ginny the cat's at Hannah's. Over at the Camp. I have to go back and get her."

Mommy: "We'll go get her tomorrow."

Tonight I'm staying at the Holiday Inn with Mommy. She took me to Walmart. We ate at McDonald's. We even swam in the big, blue swimming pool. It was so much fun.

I told Mommy, "I only wish Abraham could be here. I mean Austin."

She hugged me and we cried a little then.

She said a federal agent's going to take us up to Meadow Ridge tomorrow so I can get my clothes and things. Maybe she'll want to save some of Abraham's things to remember Austin by.

"What about Travis and little Joseph?" I asked her.

Mommy looked sad then. "All I can promise you is we'll do our very best to see they are cared for. But the law says we can't take them with us. Not right now, anyway. Someone else will have to make that decision for them."

Oh Juniper, a mom's love is truly divine. A love so strong she moved heaven and earth to find me. Until today. Now I have a real mom. And I'm going home. To Florida. We leave day after tomorrow. She still lives on Bird of Paradise Lane.

"I couldn't bear to leave that house," she told me. "In case someday you found your way back home again."

And that's exactly what I did. These letters helped me find my way back home. I will probably always write to you. But to you, as me, from now on. Like a diary. For Juniper and Sarah are really one in the same. Once I get used to the idea, it'll be fine.

You're still my best friend, as always. Especially now, because I know where you are.

Your friend,

Juniper

About the Author

Peggy Tibbetts is the author of two middle grade novels, *Letters to Juniper* and *The Road to Weird*; two young adult novels, *PFC Liberty Stryker* and *Hurricane Katrina;* and a suspense novel for adults, *Rumors of War.* She has worked as a professional editor and is a fervent blogger.

She enjoys hiking, biking, skiing, and camping with her husband, Tod and beloved Malamute, Zeus, in the mountains of western Colorado, where they live.

A Note from the Editor

Because this book was written in the viewpoint of a 12-year-old girl, we have allowed some anomalies that we would not otherwise leave in a book. To keep the "realistic" feel of a child's journal, there are some places where it does not adhere to the Chicago Manual of Style. Sisterhood Publications edits according to Chicago, but there are times when we make an exception, and this is one of them.

Made in the USA
Charleston, SC
04 June 2011